BONEHEAD
WAS THE PERFECT FORM OF SLAVERY

An implanted time-bomb only death could defuse.

Its power could reach the farthest outpost in space. And the Empire controlled the switch.

But then they killed the planet Earth—and not even Bonehead could stop the megapowered masterplan to blow the Empire into eternity.

TONGUES OF THE MOON
The Mind-Sizzling Novel by
PHILLIP JOSÉ FARMER

TONGUES OF THE MOON

PHILIP JOSÉ FARMER

A JOVE / HBJ BOOK

Two previous printings
First Jove/HBJ edition published July 1978

Printed in the United States of America

Jove/HBJ books are published by Jove Publications, Inc. (Har-
court Brace Jovanovich), 757 Third Avenue, New York, N.Y.
10017

FIREFLIES on the dark meadow of Earth . . .

The men and women looking up through the dome in the center of the crater of Eratosthenes were too stunned to cry out, and some did not understand all at once the meaning of those pinpoints on the shadowy face of the new Earth, the lights blossoming outwards, then dying. So bright they could be seen through the cloudmasses covering a large part of Europe. So bright they could be located as London, Paris, Brussels, Copenhagen, Leningrad, Rome, Reykjavik, Athens, Cairo. . . .

Then, a flare near Moscow that spread out and out and out. . . .

Some in the dome recovered more quickly than others. Scone and Broward, two of the Soviet North American officers present at the reception in honor of the South Atlantic Axis officers, acted swiftly enough to defend themselves.

Even as the Axes took off their caps and pulled small automatics and flat bombs from clips within the caps, the two Americans reached for the guns in their holsters.

Too late to do them much good if the Argentineans and South Africans nearest them had aimed at them. The Axes had no shock on their faces; they must have known what to expect. And their weapons were firing before the fastest of the Soviets could reach for the butts of their guns.

But the Axes must have had orders to kill the highest ranking Soviets first. At these the first fire was concentrated.

Marshal Kosselevsky had half-turned to his guest, Marshal Ramírez-Armstrong. His mouth was open and working, but no words came from it. Then, his eyes opened even wider as he saw the stubby gun in the Argentinean's hand. His own hand rose in a defensive, wholly futile, gesture.

Ramírez-Armstrong's gun twanged three times. Other Axes' bullets also struck the Russian. Kosselevsky clutched at his

5

paunch, and he fell face forward. The .22 calibers did not have much energy to penetrate deeply into the flesh. But they exploded on impact; they did their work well enough.

Scone and Broward took advantage of not being immediate targets. Guns in hand, they dived for the protection of a man-tall bank of instruments. Bullets struck the metal cases and exploded, for, in a few seconds, the Axes had accomplished their primary mission and were now out to complete their secondary.

Broward felt a sting on his cheek as he rolled behind the bank. He put his hand on his cheek, and, when he took it away, he saw his hand covered with blood. But his probing finger felt only a shallow of flesh. He forgot about the wound. Even if it had been more serious, he would have had no time to take care of it.

A South African stepped around the corner of the bank, firing as he came.

Broward shot twice with his .45. The dark-brown face showered into red and lost its human shape. The body to which it was now loosely attached curved backwards and fell on the floor.

"Broward!" called Scone above the twang and boom of the guns and the wharoop! of a bomb. "Can you see anything? I can't even stick my head around the corner without being shot at."

Broward looked at Scone, who was crouched at the other end of the bank. Scone's back was to Broward, but Scone's head was twisted far enough for him to see Broward out of the corner of his eye.

Even at that moment, when Broward's thoughts should have excluded everything but the fight, he could not help comparing Scone's profile to a face cut out of rock. The high bulbous forehead, thick bars of bone over the eyes, Dantesque nose, thin lips, and chin jutting out like a shelf of granite, more like a natural formation which happened to resemble a chin than anything which had taken shape in a human womb.

Ugly, massive, but strong. Nothing of panic or fear in that face; it was as steady as his voice.

Old Gibraltar-face, thought Broward for perhaps the hundredth time. But this time he did not feel dislike.

"I can't see any more than you—Colonel," he said.

Scone, still squatting, shifted around until he could bring

one eye to bear fully on Broward. It was a pale blue, so pale it looked empty, unhuman.

"Colonel?"

"Now," said Broward. "A bomb got General Mansfield and Colonels Omato and Ingrass. That gives you a fast promotion, sir."

"We'll both be promoted above this bank if an Axe lobs a bomb over," said Scone. "We have to get out of here."

"To where?"

Scone frowned—granite wrinkling—and said, "It's obvious the Axes want to do more than murder a few Soviets. They must plan on getting control of the bonephones. I know I would if I were they. If they can capture the control center, every Soviet on the Moon—except for the Chinese—is at their mercy. So . . ."

"We make a run for the BR?"

"I'm not ordering you to come with me," said Scone. "That's almost suicide. But you will give me a covering fire."

"I'll go with you, Colonel."

Scone glanced at the caduceuses on Broward's lapels, and he said, "We'll need your professional help after we clean out the Axes. No."

"You need my amateurish help now," said Broward. "As you see"—he jerked his thumb at the nearly headless Zulu—"I can handle a gun. And if we don't get to the bonephone controls first, life won't be worth living. Besides, I don't think the Axes intend taking any prisoners."

"You're right," said Scone. But he seemed hesitant.

"You're wondering why I'm falling in so quickly with your plan to wreck the control center?" said Broward. "You think I'm a Russky agent?"

"I didn't say I intended to wreck the transmitters," said Scone. "No. I know what you are. Or, I think I do. You're not a Russky. You're a . . ."

Scone stopped. Like Broward, he felt the rock floor quiver, then start shaking. And a low rumbling reached them, coming up through their feet before their ears detected it.

Scone, instead of throwing himself flat on the floor—an instinctive but useless maneuver—jumped up from his squatting position.

"Now! Now! The others'll be too scared to move!"

Broward rose, though he wanted to cling to the floor. Directly below them—or, perhaps, to the side but still underground—a white-hot "tongue" was blasting a narrow tunnel through the rock. Behind it, also hidden within the rock, in a shaft which the vessel must have taken a long time to sink without being detected, was a battlebird. Only a large ship could carry the huge generators required to drive a tongue that would damage a base. A tongue, or snake, as it was sometimes called. A flexible beam of "straightened-out" photons, the ultimate development of the laser.

And when the tongue reached the end of the determined tunnel, then the photons would be "unsprung." And all the energy crammed into the compressed photons would dissipate.

"Follow me!" said Scone, and he began running.

Broward took a step, halted in amazement, called out, "The suits . . . other way!"

Then, he resumed running after Scone. Evidently, the colonel was not concerned about the dome cracking wide open. His only thought was for the bonephone controls.

Broward expected to be cut down under a storm of bullets. But the room was silent except for the groans of some wounded. And the ever-increasing rumble from deep under.

The survivors of the fight were too intent on the menace probing beneath them to pay attention to the two runners—if they saw them.

That is, until Scone bounded through the nearest exit from the dome in a great leap afforded by the Moon's weak gravity. He almost hit his head on the edge of the doorway.

Then, somebody shot at Broward. But his body, too, was flying through the exit, his legs pulled up, and the three bullets passed beneath him and blew holes in the rock wall ahead of him.

Broward slammed into the wall and fell back on the floor. Though half-stunned, he managed to roll past the corner, out of the line of fire, into the hallway. He rose, breathing hard, and checked to make sure he had not broken his numbed wrists and hands, which had cushioned much of his impact against the wall. And he was thankful that the tongues needed generators too massive to be compacted into hand weapons. If the Axes had been able to smuggle tonguers into the dome, they could have wiped out every Soviet on the base.

The rumble became louder. The rock beneath his feet shook. The walls quivered like jelly. Then . . .

Not the ripping upwards of the floor beneath his feet, the ravening blast opening the rock and lashing out at him with sear of fire and blow of air to burn him and crush him against the ceiling at the same time.

From somewhere deep and off to one side was an explosion. The rock swelled. Then, subsided.

Silence.

Only his breathing.

For about six seconds while he thought that the Russian ships stationed outside the base must have located the sunken Axis vessel and destroyed it just before it blew up the base.

From the dome, a hell's concerto of small-gun fire.

Broward ran again, leaping over the twisted and shattered bodies of Russians and Axes. Here the attacking officers had been met by Soviet guards, and the two groups had destroyed each other.

Far down the corridor, Scone's tall body was hurtling alone, taking the giant steps only a long-time Lunie could safely handle. He rounded a corner, was gone down a branching corridor.

Broward, following Scone, entered two more branches, and then stopped when he heard the boom of a .45. Two more booms. Silence. Broward cautiously stuck his head around the corner.

He saw two Russian soldiers on the floor, their weapons close to their lifeless hands. Down the hall, Scone was running.

Broward did not understand. He could only surmise that the Russians had been so surprised by Scone that they had fired, or tried to fire, before they recognized the North American uniform. And Scone had shot in self-defense.

But the corridors were well lit with electroluminescent panels. All three should have seen at once that none wore the silver of Argentina or the scarlet and brown of the South Africans. So . . . ?

He did not know. Scone could tell him, but Broward would have trouble catching up with him.

Then, once more, he heard the echoes of a .45 bouncing around the distant corner of the hall.

When Broward rounded the turn as cautiously as he had the previous one, he saw two more dead Russians. And he saw Scone rifling the pockets of the officer of the two.

"Scone!" he shouted so the man would not shoot him, too, in a frenzy. "It's Broward!"

Coming closer, he said, "What're you doing?"

Scone rose from the officer with a thin plastic cylinder

about a decimeter long in one hand. With the other hand, he pointed his .45 at Broward's solar plexus.

"I'm going to blow up the controls and the transmitters," he said. "What did you think?"

Choking, Broward said, "You're not working for the Axis?"

He did not believe Scone was. But, in his astonishment, he could only think of that as a reason for Scone's behavior. Despite his accusation about Scone's intentions, he had not really believed the man meant to do more than insure that the controls did not fall into Axis hands.

Scone said, "Those swine! No! I'm just making sure that the Axes will not be able to use the bonephones if they do seize this office. Besides, I have never liked the idea of being under Russian control. These hellish devices . . ."

Broward pointed at the corpses. "Why?"

"They had their orders," said Scone. "Which were to allow no one into the control room without proper authorization. I didn't want to argue and so put them on their guard. I had to do what was expedient."

Scone glared at Broward, and he said, "Expediency is going to be the rule for this day. No matter who suffers."

Broward said, "You don't have to kill me, too. I am an American. If I could think as coolly as you, I might have done the same thing myself."

He paused, took a deep breath, and said, "Perhaps, you didn't do this on the spur of the moment. Perhaps, you planned this long before. If such a situation as this gave you a chance."

"We haven't time to stand here gabbing," said Scone.

He backed away, his gun and gaze steady on Broward. With his other hand, he felt around until the free end of the thin tube fitted into the depression in the middle of the door. He pressed in on the key, and (the correct sequence of radio frequencies activating the unlocking circuit) the door opened.

Scone motioned for Broward to precede him. Broward entered. Scone came in, and the door closed behind him.

"I thought I should kill you when we were behind the bank," said Scone. "But you weren't—as far as I had been able to determine—a Russian agent. Far from it. And you were as you said, a fellow American. But . . ."

Broward looked at the far wall with its array on array of indicator lights, switches, pushbuttons, and slots for admission of coded cards and tapes.

He turned to Scone, and he said, "Time for us to quit being coy. I've known for a long time that you were the chief of a Nationalist underground."

For the first time since Broward had known him, Scone's face cracked wide open.

"What?"

Then, the cracks closed up, the cliff-front was solid again.

"Why didn't you report me. Or are you. . .?"

"Not of your movement, no," said Broward. "I'm an Athenian. You've heard of us?"

"I know of them," said Scone. "A lunatic fringe. Neither Russ, Chinese, nor Yank. I had suspected that you weren't a very solid Marxist. Why tell me this?"

"I want to talk you out of destroying the controls and the transmitters," said Broward.

"Why?"

"Don't blow them up. Given time, the Russ could build another set. And we'd be under their control again. Don't destroy them. Plant a bomb which can be set off by remote control. The moment they try to use the phones to paralyze us, blow up the transmitters. That might give us time to remove the phones from our skulls with surgery. Or insulate the phones against reception. Or, maybe, strike at the Russkies. If fighting back is what you have in mind. I don't know how far your Nationalism goes."

"That might be better," said Scone, his voice flat, not betraying any enthusiasm for the plan. "Can I depend upon you and your people?"

"I'll be frank. If you intend to try for complete independence of the Russians, you'll have our wholehearted cooperation. Until we are independent."

"And after that—what then?"

"We believe in violence only after all other means have failed. Of course, mental persuasion was useless with the Russians. With fellow Americans, well . . ."

"How many people do you have at Clavius?"

Broward hesitated, then said, "Four. All absolutely dependable. Under my orders. And you?"

"More than you," said Scone. "You understand that I'm not sharing the command with you? We can't take time out to confer. We need a man who can give orders to be carried out instantly. And my word will be life or death? No argument?"

"No time now for discussions of policy. I can see that. Yes.

I place myself and my people under your orders. But what about the other Americans? Some are fanatical Marxists. Some are unknown, X."

"We'll weed out the bad ones," said Scone. "I don't mean by bad the genuine Marxists. I'm one myself. I mean the non-Nationalists. If anyone wants to go to the Russians, we let them go. Or if anybody fights us, they die."

"Couldn't we just continue to keep them prisoners?"

"On the Moon? Where every mouth needs two pairs of hands to keep breathing and eating? Where even one parasite may mean eventual death for all others? No!"

Broward said, "All right. They die. I hope . . ."

"Hopes are something to be tested," said Scone. "Let's get to work. There should be plenty of components here with which to rig up a control for the bomb. And I have the bomb taped to my belly."

You won't have to untape your bomb," said Broward. "The transmitters are mined. So are the generators."

"How did you do it? And why didn't you tell me you'd already done it?"

"The Russians have succeeded in making us Americans distrust each other," said Broward. "Like everybody else, I don't reveal information until I absolutely have to. As to your first question, I'm not only a doctor, I'm also a physical anthropologist engaged in a Moonwide project. I frequently attend conferences at this base, stay here several sleeps. And what you did so permanently with your gun, I did temporarily with a sleep-inducing aerosol. But, now that we understand each other, let's get out."

"Not until I see the bombs you say you've planted."

Broward smiled. Then, working swiftly with a screwdriver he took from a drawer, he removed several wall-panels. Scone looked into the recesses and examined the component boards, functional blocks, and wires which jammed the interior.

"I don't see any explosives," Scone said.

"Good," said Broward. "Neither will the Russians, unless they measure the closeness of the walls to the equipment. The explosive is spread out over the walls in a thin layer which is colored to match the original green. Also, thin strips of chemical are glued to the walls. This chemical is temperature-sensitive. When the transmitters are operating and reach maximum radiation of heat, the strips melt. And the chemicals released interact with the explosive, detonate it."

"Ingenious," said Scone somewhat sourly. "We don't . . ." and he stopped.

"Have such stuff? No wonder. As far as I know, the detonator and explosive were made here on the Moon. In our lab at Clavius."

"If you could get into this room without being detected and could also smuggle all that stuff from Clavius, then the Russ can be beaten," said Scone.

Now, Broward was surprised. "You doubted they could?"

"Never. But all the odds were on their side. And you know what a conditioning they give us from the day we enter kindergarten."

"Yes. The picture of the all-knowing, all-powerful Russian backed by the force of destiny itself, the inevitable rolling forward and unfolding of History as expounded by the great prophet, the only prophet, Marx. But it's not true. They're human."

They replaced the panels and the screwdriver and left the room. Just as they entered the hall, and the door swung shut behind them, they heard the thumps of boots and shouts. Scone had just straightened up from putting the key back into the dead officer's pocket when six Russians trotted around the corner. Their officer was carrying a burp gun, the others, automatic rifles.

"Don't shoot!" yelled Scone in Russian. "Americans! USAF!"

The captain, whom both Americans had seen several times before, lowered her burper.

"It's fortunate that I recognized you," she said. "We just killed three Axes who were dressed in Russian uniforms. They shot four of my men before we cut them down. I wasn't about to take a chance you might not be in disguise, too."

She gestured at the dead men. "The Axes got them, too?"

"Yes," said Scone. "But I don't know if any Axes are in there."

He pointed at the door to the control room.

"If there were, we'd all be screaming with pain," said the captain. "Anyway, they would have had to take the key from the officer on guard."

She looked suspiciously at the two, but Scone said, "You'll have to search him. I didn't touch him, of course."

She dropped to one knee and unbuttoned the officer's inner

coatpocket, which Scone had not neglected to rebutton after replacing the key.

Rising with the key, she said, "I think you two must go back to the dome."

Scone's face did not change expression at this evidence of distrust. Broward smiled slightly.

"By the way," she said, "what are you doing here?"

"We escaped from the dome," said Broward. "We heard firing down this way, and we thought we should protect our rear before going back into the dome. We found dead Russians, but we never did see the enemy. They must have been the ones you ran into."

"Perhaps," she said. "You must go. You know the rules. No unauthorized personnel near the BR."

"No non-Russians, anyway," said Scone flatly. "I know. But this is an emergency."

"You must go," she said, raising the barrel of her gun. She did not point it at them, but they did not doubt she would.

Scone turned and strode off, Broward following. When they had turned the first corner, Scone said, "We must leave the base on the first excuse. We *have* to get back to Clavius."

"So we can start our own war?"

"Not necessarily. Just declare independence. The Russ may have their belly full of death."

"Why not wait until we find out what the situation on Earth is? If the Russians have any strength left on Earth, we may be crushed."

"Now!" said Scone. "If we give the Russ and the Chinese time to recover from the shock, we lose our advantage."

"Things are going too fast for me, too," said Broward. "I haven't time or ability to think straight now. But I have thought of this. Earth could be wiped out. If so, we on the Moon are the only human beings left alive in the universe. And . . ."

"There are the Martian colonies. And the Ganymedan and Mercutian bases."

"We don't know what's happened to them. Why start something which may end the entire human species? Perhaps, ideology should be subordinated for survival. We need every man and woman, every . . ."

"We must take the chance that the Russians and Chinese won't care to risk making *Homo sapiens* extinct. They'll have to cooperate, let us go free."

"We don't have time to talk. Act now; talk after it's all over."

But Scone did not stop talking. During their passage through the corridors, he made one more statement.

"The key to peace on the Moon, and to control of this situation, is the *Zemlya*."

Broward was puzzled. He knew Scone was referring to the Brobdingnagian interstellar exploration vessel which had just been built and outfitted and was now orbiting around Earth. The *Zemlya* (Russian for Earth) had been scheduled to leave within a few days for its ten-year voyage to Alpha Centaurus and, perhaps, the stars beyond. What the *Zemlya* could have to do with establishing peace on the Moon was beyond Broward. And Scone did not seem disposed to explain.

Just then, they passed a full-length mirror, and Broward saw their images. Scone looked like a mountain of stone walking. And he, Broward thought, he himself looked like a man of leather. His shorter image, dark brown where the skin showed, his head shaven so the naked skull seemed to be overlaid with leather, his brown eyes contrasting with the rock-pale eyes of Scone, his lips too thick compared with Scone's, which were like a thin groove cut into granite. Leather against stone. Stone could outwear leather. But leather was more flexible.

Was the analogy, as so many, false? Or only partly true?

Broward tended to think in analogies; Scone, directly.

At the moment, a man like Scone was needed. Practical, quick reacting. But, like so many practical men, impractical when it came to long range and philosophical thinking. Not much at extrapolation beyond the immediate. Broward would follow him up to a point. Then . . .

They came to the entrance to the dome. Only the sound of voices came from it. Together, they stuck their heads around the side of the entrance. And they saw many dead, some wounded, a few men and women standing together near the center of the floor. All, except one, were in the variously colored and marked uniforms of the Soviet Republics. The exception was a tall man in the silver dress uniform of Argentina. His right arm hung limp, and bloody; his skin was grey.

"Colonel Lorentz," said Scone. "We've one prisoner, at least."

After shouting to those within the dome not to fire, the two walked in. Major Panchurin, the highest-ranking Russian survivor, lifted a hand to acknowledge their salute. He was too busy talking over the bonephone to say anything to them.

The two examined the dome. The visiting delegation of Axis officers was dead except for Lorentz. The Russians left standing numbered six; the Chinese, four; the Europeans, one; the Arabic, two; the Indian-East Asiatic, none. There were four Americans alive. Broward. Scone. Captain Nashdoi. And a badly wounded woman, Major Hoebel.

Broward walked towards Hoebel to examine her. Before he could do anything the Russian doctor, Titiev, rose from her side. He said, "I'm sorry, captain. She isn't going to make it."

Broward looked around the dome and made a remark which must, at the time, have seemed irrelevant to Titiev. "Only three women left. If the ratio is the same on the rest of the Moon, we've a real problem."

Scone had followed Broward. After Titiev had left, and after making sure their bonephones were not on, Scone said in a low voice, "There were seventy-five Russians stationed here. I doubt if there are over forty left in the entire base. I wonder how many in Pushkin?"

Pushkin was the base off the other side of the Moon.

They walked back to the group around Panchurin and turned on their phones so they could listen in.

Panchurin's skin paled, his eyes widened, his hands raised protestingly.

"No, no," he moaned out loud.

"What is it?" said Scone, who had heard only the last three words coming in through the device implanted in his skull.

Panchurin turned a suddenly old face to him. "The commander of the *Zemlya* said that the Argentineans have set off an undetermined number of cobalt bombs. More than twenty, at the very least."

He added, "The *Zemlya* is leaving its orbit. It intends to establish a new one around the Moon. It won't leave until we evaluate our situation. If then."

Every Soviet in the room looked at Lorentz.

The Argentinean straightened up from his weary slump

and summoned all the strength left in his bleeding body. He spoke in Russian so all would understand.

"We told you pigs we would take the whole world with us before we'd bend our necks to the Communist yoke!" he shouted.

At that moment, his gaunt high-cheekboned face with its long upper lip, thin lipline mustache, and fanatical blue eyes made him resemble the dictator of his country, Felipe Howards, El Macho (The Sledgehammer).

Panchurin ordered two soldiers and the doctor to take him to the jail. "I would like to kill the beast now," he said. "But he may have valuable information. Make sure he lives . . . for the time being."

Then, Panchurin looked upwards again to Earth, hanging only a little distance above the horizon. The others also stared.

Earth, dark now, except for steady glares here and there, forest fires and cities, probably, which would burn for days. Perhaps weeks. Then, when the fires died out, the embers cooled, no more fire. No more vegetation, no more animals, no more human beings. Not for centuries.

Suddenly, Panchurin's face crumpled, tears flowed, and he began sobbing loudly, rackingly.

The others could not withstand this show of grief. They understood now. The shock had worn off enough to allow sorrow to have its way. Grief ran through them like fire through the forests of their native homes.

Broward, also weeping, looked at Scone and could not understand. Scone, alone among the men and women under the dome and the Earth, was not crying. His face was as impassive as the slope of a Moon mountain.

Scone did not wait for Panchurin to master himself, to think clearly. He said, "I request permission to return to Clavius, sir."

Panchurin could not speak; he could only nod his head.

"Do you know what the situation is at Clavius?" said Scone relentlessly.

Panchurin managed a few words. "Some missiles . . . Axis base . . . came close . . . but no damage . . . intercepted."

Scone saluted, turned, and beckoned to Broward and Nashdoi. They followed him to the exit to the field. Here Scone made sure that the air-retaining and gamma-ray and sun-deflecting force field outside the dome was on. Then the North Americans stepped outside onto the field without their spacesuits. They had done this so many times they no longer felt the fear and helplessness first experienced upon venturing from the protecting walls into what seemed empty space. They entered their craft, and Scone took over the controls.

After identifying himself to the control tower, Scone lifted the dish and brought it to the very edge of the force field. He put the controls on automatic, the field disappeared for the two seconds necessary for the craft to pass the boundary, and the dish, impelled by its own power and by the push of escaping air, shot forward.

Behind them, the faint flicker indicating the presence of the field returned. And the escaped air formed brief and bright streamers that melted under the full impact of the sun.

"That's something that will have to be rectified in the future," said Scone. "It's an inefficient, air-wasting method. We're not so long on power we can use it to make more air every time a dish enters or leaves a field."

He returned on the r-t, contacted Clavius, told them they were coming in. To the operator, he said, "Pei, how're things going?"

"We're still at battle stations, sir. Though we doubt if there will be any more attacks. Both the Argentinean and South African bases were wrecked. They don't have any retaliatory capabilities, but survivors may be left deep underground. We've received no order from Eratosthenes to dispatch searchers to look for survivors. The base at Pushkin doesn't answer. It must . . ."

There was a crackling and a roar. When the noise died down, a voice in Russian said, "This is Eratosthenes. You will refrain from further radio communication until permission is received to resume. Acknowledge."

"Colonel Scone on the United Soviet Americas Force destroyer *Broun*. Order acknowledged."

He flipped the switch off. To Broward, he said, "Damn Russkies are starting to clamp down already. But they're rattled. Did you notice I was talking to Pei in English, and they didn't say a thing about that? I don't think they'll take much effective action or start any witch-hunts until they recover fully from the shock and have a chance to evaluate.

"Tell me, is Nashdoi one of you Athenians?"

Broward looked at Nashdoi, who was slumped on a seat at

the other end of the bridge. She was not within earshot of a low voice.

"No," said Broward. "I don't think she's anything but a lukewarm Marxist. She's a member of the Party, of course. Who on the Moon isn't? But like so many scientists here, she takes a minimum interest in ideology, just enough not to be turned down when she applied for psychological research here.

"She was married, you know. Her husband was called back to Earth only a little while ago. No one knew if it was for the reasons given or if he'd done something to displease the Russkies or arouse their suspicions. You know how it is. You're called back, and maybe you're never heard of again."

"What other way is there?" said Scone. "Although I don't like the Russky dictating the fate of any American."

"Yes?" said Broward. He looked curiously at Scone, thinking of what a mass of contradictions, from his viewpoint, existed inside that massive head. Scone believed thoroughly in the Soviet system except for one feature. He was a Nationalist; he wanted an absolutely independent North American republic, one which would reassert its place as the strongest in the world.

And that made him dangerous to the Russians and the Chinese.

America had fallen prey more to its own softness and confusion than to the machinations of the Soviets. Then, in the turbulent bloody starving years that followed the fall with their purges, uprisings, savage repressions, mass transportations to Siberia and other areas, importation of other nationalities to create division and bludgeoning propaganda and re-education, only the strong and the intelligent survived.

Scone, Broward, and Nashdoi were of the second generation born after the fall of Canada and the United States. They had been born and had lived because their parents were flexible, hardy, and quick. And because they had inherited and improved these qualities.

The Americans had become a problem to the Russians. And to the Chinese. Those Americans transported to Siberia had, together with other nationalities brought to that area, performed miracles with the harsh climate and soil, had made a garden. But they had become Siberians, not too friendly with the Russians.

China, to the south, looking for an area in which to

dump their excess population, had protested at the bringing in of other nationalities. Russia's refusal to permit Chinese entry had been one more added to the long list of grievances felt by China towards her elder brother in the Marx family.

And on the North American continent, the American Communists had become another trial to Moscow. Russia, rich with loot from the U.S., had become fat. The lean underfed hungry Americans, using the Party to work within, had alarmed the Russians with their increasing power and influence. Moreover, America had recovered, was again a great industrial empire. Ostensibly under Russian control, the Americans were pushing and pressuring subtly, and not so subtly, to get their own way. Moscow had to resist being Uncle Samified.

To complicate the world picture, thousands of North Americans had taken refuge during the fall of their country in Argentina. And there the energetic and tough-minded Yanks (the soft and foolish died on the way or after reaching Argentina) followed the paths of thousands of Italians and Germans who had fled there long ago. They became rich and powerful; Felipe Howards, El Macho, was part-Argentinean Spanish, part-German, part-American.

Recently, the South African Confederation had formed an alliance with Argentina. And the Axis had warned the Soviets that they must cease all underground activity in Axis countries, cease at once the terrible economic pressures and discriminations against them, and treat them as full partners in the nations of the world.

If this were not done and if a war started, and the Argentineans saw their country was about to be crushed, they would explode cobalt bombs.

The Soviets knew the temper of the proud and arrogant Argentineans. They had seemed to capitulate. There was a conference among the heads of the leading Soviets and Axes. Peaceful coexistence was being talked about.

But, apparently, the Axis had not swallowed this phrase as others had once swallowed it. And they had decided on a desperate move.

Having cheap lithium bombs and photon compressors and the means to deliver them with gravitomagnetic drives, the Axis was as well armed as their foes. Perhaps (their thought must have been) if they delivered the first blow, their antimissiles could intercept enough Soviet missiles so that the few that did get through would do a minimum of damage. Perhaps. No one really knew what caused the Axis to start the war.

Whatever the decision of the Axis, it had put on a good show. One of its features was the visit by their Moon officers to the base at Eratosthenes, the first presumably, in a series of reciprocal visits and parties to toast the new amiable relations.

Result: a dying Earth and a torn Moon.

Broward belonged to that small underground which neither believed in the old Soviet nor the old capitalist system. It wanted a form of government based on the ancient Athenian method of democracy on the local level and a loose confederation on the world level. All national boundaries would be abolished.

Such considerations, thought Broward, must be put aside for the time being. Getting independence of the Russians, getting rid of the hellish bonephones, was the thing to do now. Or so it had seemed to him.

But would not that inevitably lead to war and the destruction of all of humanity? Would it not be better to work with the other Soviets and hope that eventually the Communist ideal could be subverted and the Athenian established? With communities so small, the modified Athenian form of government would be workable. Later, after the Moon colonies increased in size and population, means could be found for working out intercolonial problems.

Or perhaps, thought Broward, watching the monolithic Scone, Scone did not really intend to force the other Soviets to cooperate? Perhaps, he hoped they would fight to the death and the North American base alone would be left to repopulate the world.

"Broward," said Scone, "go sound out Nashdoi. Do it subtly."

"Wise as the serpent, subtle as the dove," said Broward. "Or is it the other way around?"

Scone lifted his eyebrows. "Never heard that before. From what book?"

Broward walked away without answering. It was significant that Scone did not know the source of the quotation. The Old and New Testaments were allowed reading only for select scholars. Broward had read an illegal copy, had put his freedom and life in jeopardy by reading it.

But that was not the point here. The thought that occurred

to him was that, nationality and race aside, the people on the Moon were a rather homogeneous group. Three-fourths of them were engineers or scientists of high standing, therefore, had high I.Q.'s. They were descended from ancestors who had proved their toughness and good genes by surviving through the last hundred years. They were all either agnostics or atheists or supposed to be so. There would not be any religious differences to split them. They were all in superb health, otherwise they would not be here. No diseases among them, not even the common cold. They would all make good breeding stock. Moreover, with recent advances in genetic manipulation, defective genes could be eliminated electrochemically. Such a manipulation had not been possible on Earth with its vast population where babies were being born faster than defective genes could be wiped out. But here where there were so few . . .

Perhaps, it would be better to allow the Soviet system to exist for now. Later, use subtle means to bend it towards the desired goal.

No! The system was based on too many falsities, among which the greatest was dialectical materialism. As long as the corrupt base existed, the structure would be corrupt.

Broward sat down by Ingrid Nashdoi. She was a short, dark-skinned, small-boned, slightly overweight woman. She had light brown, very large eyes, very long eyelashes, and straight dark brown hair, cut short. Her face was a little too broad; her cheekbones were high. Although not pretty, she was considered attractive because of her vivacity, intelligence, and wit. Now, she stared at the floor, her face wooden.

Like a wooden Indian, thought Broward. Which was a natural comparison. She was half-Swedish, half-Navaho, a type of mixture not rare in these days. The Russians, during the past fifty years, had removed entire peoples from their native lands and placed them as colonists in barren countries for "redeemist" experiments. One of the areas that had seen a wholesale mixing of such nationalities and races as Swedes, New Zealanders, Turks, Peruvians, Thai, and so forth was the former Navaho-Hopi reservation of Arizona and New Mexico. Once a desert, it was now—rather, had been—a garden of farms that owed its green state to reprocessing of the surface into soil and a plentiful flow of de-ionized ocean water.

Broward and Nashdoi had grown up in the same neighborhood and attended the same secondary and primary schools.

Then, they had gone their own ways, to opposite ends of
Earth. Years later, they had met again, on the Moon. Broward
had sharpened his rusty knowledge of Navaho speech by
practicing it with her and her husband whenever he got a
chance.

"I'm sorry about Jim," he said. "But we don't have time to
grieve now. Later, perhaps."

She did not look at him but replied in a low halting voice.
"He may have been dead before the war started. I never
even got to say goodbye to him. You know what that
means. What it probably did mean."

"I don't think they got anything out of him. Otherwise, you
and I would have been arrested, too."

He jerked his head towards Scone and said, "He doesn't
know you're one of us. I want him to think you're a candidate
for the Nationalists. After this struggle with the Russ is over,
we may need someone who can report on him. Think you can
do it?"

She nodded her head, and Broward returned to Scone.
"She hates the Russians," he said. "You know they took
her husband away. She doesn't know why. But she hates
Ivan's guts."

"Good. Ah, here we go."

After the destroyer had berthed at Clavius, and the
three entered the base, events went swiftly if not smoothly.
Scone talked to the entire personnel over the IP, told them
what had happened. Then he went to his office and issued
orders to have the arsenal cleaned out of all portable weapons. These were transferred to the four destroyers the Russians had assigned to Clavius as a token force.

Broward then called in his four Athenians and Scone, his
five Nationalists. The situation was explained to them, and
they were informed of what was expected of them. Even Broward was startled, but didn't protest.

After the weapons had been placed in the destroyers,
Scone ordered the military into his office one at a time. And,
one at a time, they were disarmed and escorted by another
door to the arsenal and locked in. Three of the soldiers asked
to join Scone, and he accepted two. Several protested furiously and denounced Scone as a traitor.

Then, Scone had the civilians assembled in the large
auditorium (Technically, all personnel were in the military,
but the scientists were only used in that capacity during
emergencies.) Here, he told them what he had done, what

he planned to do—except for one thing—and asked them if they wished to enlist. Again, he got a violent demonstration from some and sullen silence from others. These were locked up in the arsenal.

The others were sworn in, except for one man. Whiteside. Broward pointed him out as an agent and informer for both the Russians and Chinese. Scone admitted that he had not known about the triple-dealer, but he took Broward's word and had Whiteside locked up, too.

Then, the radios of the two scout ships were smashed, and the prisoners marched out and jammed into them. Scone told them they were free to fly to the Russian base. Within a few minutes, the scouts hurtled away from Clavius towards the north.

"But, Colonel," said Broward, "they can't give the identifying code to the Russians. They'll be shot down."

"They are traitors; they prefer the Russky to us. Better for us if they are shot down. They'll not fight for Ivan."

Broward did not have much appetite when he sat down to eat and to listen to Scone's detailing of his plan.

"The *Zemlya*," he said, "has everything we need to sustain us here. And to clothe the Earth with vegetation and replace her animal life in the distant future when the radiation is low enough for us to return. Her deepfreeze tanks contain seeds and plants of thousands of different species of vegetation. They also hold, in suspended animation, the bodies of cattle, sheep, horses, rabbits, dogs, cats, fowl, birds, useful insects and worms. The original intention was to reanimate these and use them on any Terrestrial-type planet the *Zemlya* might find.

"Now our bases here are self-sustaining. But, when the time comes to return to Earth, we must have vegetation and animals. Otherwise, what's the use?

"So, whoever holds the *Zemlya* holds the key to the future. We must be the ones who hold that key. With it, we can bargain; the Russians and the Chinese will have to agree to independence if they want to share in the seeds and livestock."

"What if the *Zemlya's* commander chooses destruction of his vessel rather than surrender?" said Broward. "Then, all of humanity will be robbed. We'll have no future."

"I have a plan to get us aboard the *Zemlya* without violence."

An hour later, the four USAF destroyers accelerated outwards towards Earth. Their radar had picked up the *Zemlya;* it also had detected five other Unidentified Space Objects. These were the size of their own craft.

Abruptly, the *Zemlya* radioed that it was being attacked. Then, silence. No answer to the requests from Eratosthenes for more information.

Scone had no doubt about the attackers' identity. "The Axis leaders wouldn't have stayed on Earth to die," he said. "They'll be on their way to their big base on Mars. Or, more likely, they have the same idea as us. Capture the *Zemlya.*"

"And if they do?" said Broward.

"We take it from them."

The four vessels continued to accelerate in the great curve which would take them out away from the *Zemlya* and then would bring them around towards the Moon again. Their path was computed to swing them around so they would come up behind the interstellar ship and overtake it. Though the titanic globe was capable of eventually achieving far greater speeds than the destroyers, it was proceeding at a comparatively slow velocity. This speed was determined by the orbit around the Moon into which the *Zemlya* intended to slip.

In ten hours, the USAF complement had curved around and were about 10,000 kilometers from the *Zemlya.* Their speed was approximately 20,000 kilometers an hour at this point, but they were decelerating. The Moon was bulking larger; ahead of them, visible by the eye, were two steady gleams. The *Zemlya* and the only Axis vessel which had not been blown to bits or sliced to fragments. According to the *Zemlya,* which was again in contact with the Russian base, the Axis ship had been cut in two by a tongue from *Zemlya.*

But the interstellar ship was now defenseless. It had launched every missile and anti-missile in its arsenal. And the fuel for the tongue-generators was exhausted.

"Furthermore," said Shaposhnikov, commander of the *Zemlya,* "new USO has been picked up on the radar. Four coming in from Earth. If these are also Axis, then the *Zemlya* has only two choices. Surrender. Or destroy itself."

"There is nothing we can do," replied Eratosthenes. "But we do not think those USO are Axis. We detected four destroyer-sized objects leaving the vicinity of the USAF base, and we asked them for identification. They did not answer, but we have reason to believe they are North American."

"Perhaps they are coming to our rescue," suggested Shaposhnikov.

"They left before anyone knew you were being attacked. Besides, they had no orders from us."

"What do I do?" said Shaposhnikov.

Scone, who had tapped into the tight laser beam, broke it up by sending random pulses into it. The *Zemlya* discontinued its beam, and Scone then sent them a message through a pulsed tongue which the Russian base could tap into only through a wild chance.

After transmitting the proper code identification, Scone said, "Don't renew contact with Eratosthenes. It is held by the Axis. They're trying to lure you close enough to grab you. We escaped the destruction of our base. Let me aboard where we can confer about our next step. Perhaps, we may have to go to Alpha Centaurus with you."

For several minutes, the *Zemlya* did not answer. Shaposhnikov must have been unnerved. Undoubtedly, he was in a quandary. In any case, he could not prevent the strangers from approaching. If they were Axis, they had him at their mercy.

Such must have been his reasoning. He replied, "Come ahead."

By then, the USAF dishes had matched their speeds to that of the *Zemlya's*. From a distance of only a kilometer, the sphere looked like a small Earth. It even had the continents painted on the surface, though the effect was spoiled by the big Russian letters painted on the Pacific Ocean.

Scone gave a lateral thrust to his vessel, and it nudged gently into the enormous landing-port of the sphere. Within five minutes, his crew of ten were in the control room.

Scone did not waste any time. He drew his gun; his men followed suit; he told Shaposhnikov what he meant to do. The Russian, a tall thin man of about fifty, seemed numbed. Perhaps, too many catastrophes had happened in too short a time. The death of Earth, the attack by the Axis ships, and, now, totally unexpected, this. The world was coming to an end in too many shapes and too swiftly.

Scone cleared the control room of all *Zemlya* personnel except the commander. The others were locked up with the forty-odd men and women who were surprised at their posts by the Americans.

Scone ordered Shaposhnikov to set up orders to the navigational computer for a new path. This one would send the

Zemlya at maximum acceleration towards a point in the south polar region near Clavius. When the *Zemlya* reached the proper distance, it would begin a deceleration which would bring it to a halt approximately half a kilometer above the surface at the intended area.

Shaposhnikov, speaking disjointedly like a man coming up out of a nightmare, protested that the *Zemlya* was not built to stand such a strain. Moreover, if Scone succeeded in his plan to hide the great globe at the bottom of a chasm under an overhang . . . Well, he could only predict that the lower half of the *Zemlya* would be crushed under the weight—even with the Moon's weak gravity.

"That won't harm the animal tanks," said Scone. "They're in the upper levels. Do as I say. If you don't, I'll shoot you and set up the computer myself."

"You are mad," said Shaposhnikov. "But I will do my best to get us down safely. If this were ordinary war, if we weren't man's—Earth's—last hope, I would tell you to go ahead, shoot. But . . ."

Ingrid Nashdoi, standing beside Broward, whispered in a trembling voice, "The Russian is right. He is mad. It's too great a gamble. If we lose, then everybody loses."

"Exactly what Scone is betting on," murmured Broward. "He knows the Russians and Chinese know it, too. Like you, I'm scared. If I could have foreseen what he was going to do, I think I'd have put a bullet in him back at Eratosthenes. But it's too late to back out now. We go along with him no matter what."

The voyage from the Moon and the capture of the *Zemlya* had taken twelve hours. Now, with the *Zemlya's* mighty drive applied—and the four destroyers riding in the landing-port —the voyage back took three hours. During this time, the Russian base sent messages. Scone refused to answer. He intended to tell all the Moon his plans but not until the *Zemlya* was close to the end of its path. When the globe was a thousand kilometers from the surface, and decelerating with the force of 3g's, he and his men returned to the destroyers. All except three, who remained with Shaposhnikov.

The destroyers streaked ahead of the *Zemlya* towards an entrance to a narrow canyon. This led downwards to a chasm where Scone intended to place the *Zemlya* beneath a giant overhang.

But, as the four sped towards the opening two crags, their

radar picked up four objects coming over close to the mountains to the north. A battlebird and three destoyers. Scone knew that the Russians had another big craft and three more destroyers available. But they probably did not want to send them out, too, and leave the base comparatively defenseless.

He at once radioed the commander of the *Lermontov* and told him what was going on.

"We declare independence, a return to Nationalism," he concluded. "And we call on the other bases to do the same."

The commander roared, "Unless you surrender at once, we turn on the bonephones! And you will writhe in pain until you die, you American swine!"

"Do that little thing," said Scone, and he laughed.

He switched on the communication beams linking the four ships and said, "Hang on for a minute or two, men. Then, it'll be all over. For us and for them."

Two minutes later, the pain began. A stroke of heat like lighting that seemed to sear the brains in their skulls. They screamed, all except Scone, who grew pale and clutched the edge of the control panel. But the dishes were, for the next two minutes, on automatic, unaffected by their pilots' condition.

And then, just as suddenly as it had started, the pain died. They were left shaking and sick, but they knew they would not feel that unbearable agony again.

"Flutter your craft as if it's going out of control," said Scone. "Make it seem we're crashing into the entrance to the canyon."

Scone himself put the lead destroyer through the simulation of a craft with a pain-crazed pilot at the controls. The others followed his maneuvers, and they slipped into the canyon.

From over the top of the cliff to their left rose a glare that would have been intolerable if the plastic over the portholes had not automatically polarized to dim the brightness.

Broward, looking through a screen which showed the view to the rear, cried out. Not because of the light from the atomic bomb which had exploded on the other side of the cliff. He yelled because the top of the *Zemlya* had also lit up. And he knew in that second what had happened. The light did not come from the warhead, for an extremely high mountain was between the huge globe and the blast. If the upper region of the *Zemlya* glowed, it was because a tongue from a Russian ship had brushed against it.

It must have been an accident, for the Russians surely had no wish to wreck the *Zemlya*. If they defeated the USAF, they could recapture the globe with no trouble.

"My God, she's falling!" yelled Broward. "Out of control!"

Scone looked once and quickly. He turned away and said, "All craft land immediately. All personnel transfer to my ship."

The maneuver took three minutes, for the men in the other dishes had to connect air tanks to their suits and then run from their ships to Scone's. Moreover, one man in each destroyer was later than his fellows since he had to set up the controls on his craft.

Scone did not explain what he meant to do until all personnel had made the transfer. In the meantime, they were at the mercy of the Russians if the enemy had chosen to attack over the top of the cliff. But Scone was gambling that the Russians would be too horrified at what was happening to the *Zemlya*. His own men would have been frozen if he had not compelled them to act. The Earth dying twice within twenty-four hours was almost more than they could endure.

Only the American commander, the man of stone, seemed not to feel.

Scone took his ship up against the face of the cliff until she was just below the top. Here the cliff was thin because of the slope on the other side. And here, hidden from view of the Russians, he drove a tongue two decimeters wide through the rock.

And, at the moment three Russian destroyers hurtled over the edge, tongues of compressed light lashing out on every side in the classic flailing movement, Scone's beam broke through the cliff.

The three empty USAF ships, on automatic, shot upwards at a speed that would have squeezed their human occupants into jelly—if they had had occupants. Their tongues shot out and flailed, caught the Russian tongues.

Then, the American vessels rammed into the Russians, drove them upwards, flipped them over. And all six craft fell along the cliff's face, Russian and American intermingled, crashing into each other, bouncing off the sheer face, exploding, their fragments colliding, and smashed into the bottom of the canyon.

Scone did not see this, for he had completed the tongue through the tunnel, turned it off for a few seconds, and sent a video beam through. He was just in time to see the big battlebird start to float off the ground where it had been waiting. Perhaps, it had not accompanied the destroyers because of Russian contempt for American ability. Or, perhaps, because the commander was under orders not to risk the big ship unless necessary. Even now, the *Lermontov* rose slowly as if it might take two paths: over the cliff or towards the *Zemlya*. But, as it rose, Scone applied full power.

Some one, or some detecting equipment, on the *Lermontov* must have caught view of the tongue as it slid through space to intercept the battlebird. A tongue shot out towards the American beam. Then Scone's was in contact with the hull, and a hole appeared in the irradiated plastic.

Majestically, the *Lermontov* continued rising—and so cut itself almost in half. And, majestically, it fell.

Not before the Russian commander touched off all the missiles aboard his ship in a last frenzied defense, and the missiles flew out in all directions. Two hit the slope, blew off the face of the mountain on the *Lermontov*'s side, and a jet of atomic energy flamed out through the tunnel created by Scone.

But he had dropped his craft like an elevator, was halfway down the cliff before the blasts made his side of the mountain tremble.

Half an hour later, the base of Eratosthenes sued for peace. For the sake of human continuity, said Panchurin, all fighting must cease forever on the Moon.

The Chinese, who had been silent up to then despite their comrades' pleas for help, also agreed to accept the policy of Nationalism.

Now, Broward expected Scone to break down, to give way to the strain. He would only have been human if he had done so.

He did not. Not, at least, in anyone's presence.

Broward awoke early during a sleep-period. Unable to forget the dream he had just had, he went to find Ingrid Nashdoi. She was not in her lab; her assistant told him that she had gone to the dome with Scone.

Jealous, Broward hurried there and found the two standing there and looking up at the half-Earth. Ingrid was holding a puppy in her arms. This was one of the few animals that had been taken unharmed from the shattered tanks of the fallen *Zemlya*.

Broward, looking at them, thought of the problems that faced the Moon people. There was that of government, though this seemed for the moment to be settled. But he knew that there would be more conflict between the bases and that his own promotion of the Athenian ideology would cause grave trouble.

There was also the problem of women. One woman to every three men. How would this be solved? Was there any answer other than heartaches, frustration, hate, even murder?

"I had a dream," said Broward to them. "I dreamed that we on the Moon were building a great tower which would reach up to the Earth and that was our only way to get back to Earth. But everybody spoke a different tongue, and we couldn't understand each other. Therefore, we kept putting the bricks in the wrong places or getting into furious but unintelligible argument about construction."

He stopped, saw they expected more, and said, "I'm sorry. That's all there was. But the moral is obvious."

"Yes," said Ingrid, stroking the head of the wriggling puppy. She looked up at Earth, close to the horizon. "The physicists say it'll be two hundred years before we can go back. Do you realize that, barring accident or war, all three of us might live to see that day? That we might return with our great-great-great-great-great-great-great grandchildren? And we can tell them of the Earth that was, so they will know how to build the Earth that must be."

"Two hundred years?" said Broward. "We won't be the same persons then."

But he doubted that even the centuries could change Scone. The man was made of rock. He would not bend or flow. Broward felt sorry for him. He would be a fossil, truly a stone man, a petrified hero.

"We'll never get back unless we do today's work every day," said Scone. "I'll worry about Earth when it's time to worry. Let's go; we've work to do."

Broward was walking down a corridor when he felt the rock beneath his feet tremble. Far, far below him, a battery of lasers was drilling into the depths of the Moon. Primarily, the drillers were looking for water, and they were sure that they were headed for a huge pocket of the liquid in one form or another. Secondarily, hollowing out tunnels would increase the *Lebensraum* for the inhabitants of Clavius. Some day, the population would be large enough to need that extra room.

That is, thought Broward, it would if the survivors of mankind could agree on a means of keeping peace. At the moment, that did not seem very likely.

He stopped before a door and spoke into the outline of a square set above a blank screen. It sprang into life; Ingrid Nashdoi's features appeared on it. Seeing Broward, she smiled and brushed back a lock of light brown hair hanging over one forehead.

Like all on the Clavian base, she had a small circular area on the right side of her head where the hair had been shaved off before the bonephone was removed.

Broward walked in, looked around, and said, "Where's Miller?"

"Scone called a meeting. As a matter of fact, he came here to tell Miller he was wanted. I don't know why he didn't use the com."

Broward grinned sourly. Ingrid said, "I hate myself. I'm not being honest. And I'm not fooling you. Scone is interested in me. I guess everybody knows that. Accept my apologies?"

"That's one reason I love you," said Broward. "You're honest."

"My! How popular I've suddenly become! You're the second man who's told me that today."

"The other one was Scone?"

Ingrid laughed and said, "Hardly! Do you think Scone would put himself in a position to be rejected? No, if he asks me to marry him. he'll do so when he's dead sure that I won't or can't refuse."

"I wonder why Scone didn't tell me there was a meeting?" said Broward.

"You didn't hear a word I was saying. You don't really love me."

Broward said, "I wish I thought you really cared. But . . ."

"Scone called a meeting of the scientists who are responsible for our food supply. He did say something to Miller about Miller's also being present at a policy meeting later. I imagine you won't be left out of that."

Broward looked relieved. He smiled and said, "Who was the other man, Ingrid?"

"What other man? Oh . . . you mean . . .? Well, that's a private affair. However, I expect others soon. It won't be so flattering, though. It's just that . . . well, when cows are scarce, the price is high."

"What?"

"There are three and a half men to every woman on the Moon," replied Ingrid. "Don't ask me how the statisticians account for all those half-men walking around without heads or arms. Can't you just see them?"

She laughed; Broward grinned slightly. He said, "It's very serious. We have to increase the population, and we must use all the genes available. Can't have inbreeding, you know."

"I'm a psychologist," she said, "but it doesn't need a psychologist to predict trouble ahead. I overheard Doctor Abarbanel yesterday. You know her, the tall, many-curved, dark-haired, thick-lipped, disgustingly sultry biochemist? She said that the women on the base will just have to get used to group-marriage. She seemed to like the idea."

"She was serious?"

"Why shouldn't she be? You have any better ideas?"

"Not at present," said Broward. "I don't like the idea though. What about Scone? He'd never sanction it. He's a strict moralist, at least in sexual matters. When it comes to spilling blood, that's something else."

"I don't know. I do know something Abarbanel didn't think of. That is, whether or not we have polygamy, a woman isn't always going to bear children by whomever she chooses. The gene potential will have to be used. So, that means that if a woman has three children—and I doubt that they'll allow us to limit ourselves—each will have a different father. Of course, there's artificial insemination, so . . . What's the matter? You look upset."

"I couldn't stand the idea of you . . . that is . . ."

Ingrid came up to him, put her hands on his shoulders, and looked carefully at him. "If you were serious a moment ago, why don't you say so?"

He took her into his arms, kissed her a long time. Then, releasing her, he said, "I've known for about a week that I loved you, Ingrid. But I didn't think that now was the time to start courting. There's too much to do just now; things are too uncertain."

She gave a little laugh and said, "'If all men were like you in times of trouble, the human race would be extinct. People don't wait until they're sure the bombs are going to quit bursting. Why do you think that, despite the millions killed, there were more people on Earth at the end of the Second World War than there were when it started?"

"I don't like to start anything I'm not sure I can finish."

"In some ways, you're worse than Scone," she said. "But I love you."

"I don't want to share you with any other men," he said fiercely.

"I'm glad you don't. I wouldn't like it if you said it was all right, it was for the glory of the state and humankind. But . . ."

"But what?" said Broward. Ingrid opened her mouth but closed it when Broward's name was announced over the IP. He listened, then said, "This is what I've been waiting for. Scone is going to brief us on the meeting with the representatives from the other bases."

"They're coming *here*? How did he manage that?"

"He holds the key to the future of man. The *Zemlya*. The Russ and the Chinese have to play along with him. But I don't think Scone is going to get what he wants without a long hard struggle."

Clavius is a crater near the south pole of the Moon. It is so wide across that a man standing on its floor in the center cannot even see its towering walls; they are hidden beyond the curve of the horizon. And the Earth always hangs just a little above the horizon. It was towards the Earth that those first entering the conference looked. They could not help it, for Scone had had the ceiling and one wall depolarized for transparency, and those within the room could see the great globe. Their first thought was what Scone had wanted; the dead Earth made sure of that. *All life there is gone, and we are the survivors. It is up to us to ensure that life does not die entirely in the solar system.*

The room itself was carved out of rock and normally was used for recreation. Now, the gaming machines and tables had been pushed against the wall and about a hundred aluminum folding chairs were arranged in rows facing the platform. On this was a large rectangular table with eleven chairs which faced the audience. Scone sat in the middle chair. Immediately on his right was Dahlquist, the Swedish linguist, delegate of the West Europeans (all of whom had taken refuge in Clavius after their base was wrecked). The four Russian delegates sat on Scone's right; the Chinese, on his left.

For a while, there was much shuffling around and talking in low tones, then Old Man Dahlquist, so-called because he was senior by many years to anybody else on the Moon, rose.

He rapped once with a gavel and then spoke in flawless Midwestern English.

"Ladies and gentlemen, I introduce to you the chairman of this meeting, Colonel Scone."

Scone rose and looked around. There was no applause. He opened his mouth, but before he could say anything, John Ying, a Chinese delegate, jumped to his feet and spoke excitedly in Mandarin.

"I protest! Under what authority does . . . ?"

Scone bellowed at him. "Sit down! You accepted my invitation to attend this meeting, and you were told why you are here! I am chairman, and I will waste no time disputing my right to be so nor the reason for this conference! Moreover, during this conference, no one who speaks in anything but English will be recognized. Sit down and shut up until I give you permission to speak!"

Broward, sitting in the front row of the audience, thought that Scone was being very arrogant indeed. Yet, he could not help being pleased. The North Americans had suffered much after the war when the Chinese had occupied the western coast. Later, the Russians had forced withdrawal of all the Chinese except a few token garrisons. The Russians were no better, but the westerners had not forgotten their savage treatment by the Orientals.

Ying was red in the face, quivering, his fists clenched. He glared at Scone, but Scone regarded him with a face as immovable as that of Mount Everest. Presently, Ying sat down.

"Now," said Scone. "Everyone in this room has been given a document. This outlines the reasons for our being here. Also, the rules by which we will proceed. If you don't care to attend or to obey the parliamentary rules, leave now."

He paused and stared around the room. Seeing that no one was disposed to take action, he said, "Very well. The first thing we should take into consideration is the military aspect. That is, the type of action to be taken against the Axis colonies on Mars, if there are any left, and what type of organization we will operate with.

"Unfortunately, there are other matters to be cleared up before we can discuss that. The main thing is, which base will be the leader? I say leader, not equal partner, because I know what will happen if we have a joint military head. With three commanders-in-chief, all with equal powers, we will have nothing but quarreling over matters of policy and ways to implement that policy. To survive, we must have one unquestioned leader, a man who can decide at once what action to take. And who will be obeyed without hesitation.

"Since we of Clavius hold the whip hand, and since I am the commander of Clavius, I will be the commander-in-chief."

He paused again to look at the shocked men at the table with him.

Broward, though he felt uncomfortable at the brutal directness of Scone and his arrogance, was also pleased. To see the situation now reversed, the Americans giving the orders and the Russians and Chinese helpless to do anything about it, warmed him.

Ying said, "Colonel Scone."

"You will address me as Mr. Chairman."

Ying swallowed and said, "Mr. Chairman."

"You may speak, General Ying."

"You Clavians need us as much as we need you. Therefore . . ."

"You are wrong, General. We need you, but not as much as you need us. Not nearly as much. You know that. Let's have no more argument on that point."

Ying closed his eyes, and his lips moved silently.

Scone smiled slightly. He said, "Russian *was* the means for intercommunication between the bases. It will now be English. And this brings up another matter. Language is not only a means for communication. It may also be a barrier to communication. I foresee that we will all become one people in the future, a long time before we or our descendants are able to return to Earth. The use of three or more languages will keep us separate, maintain the hostilities and misunderstandings. I propose, therefore, that we make one language the primary tongue of all. Our children will be taught this language, will grow up thinking of it as their native tongue."

Broward rose. "Mr. Chairman!"

"Captain Broward."

"I move that all the bases of the Moon should agree to accept one language as the primary language. This will be spoken everywhere, except in the privacy of one's quarters, where one may use whatever language pleases him."

Miller, the zoologist, rose and seconded the motion.

Scone then declared that the representatives and delegates could speak for their choices. Each speaker was to be limited to two minutes, and a particular language could not be pled for more than once.

Panchurin, the Russian commandant, was the first to be

recognized. He was a short broad man with brown-yellow hair and a broad high cheekboned face and was thirty-five years old.

"I do not understand how English can be made the language of base intercommunication but some other language can also be the universal speech. There is a contradiction."

"English will be used during the present state of emergency. Afterwards, we will adopt whichever tongue is chosen at this meeting. Let me remind you what I told you in the document. That is, that the voting on various issues will not be a farce. I have not, as they say in English, packed the house. For every American or West European at this meeting, there is a Russian and a Chinese."

Broward smiled. It was true that the Russian and Chinese bases had a number of delegates to equal those of Clavius. But they had sent only those specifically invited by Scone. And he had included among the Russian nationals various Turkish speakers, Armenians, Georgians, Lithuanians, Estonians. And among the Chinese were several Japanese, Indonesians, Indians, Thai, and Filipinos, none of whom had any reason to love the Chinese.

Panchurin said, "Then I understand correctly that the universal language will be chosen by popular vote? That the particular one will not be rammed down our throats?"

"Of course not. I am only requiring that we vote on one now because, after the Axis have been dealt with, we may not be able to agree so easily or quickly on an issue like this."

"I would speak of the Russian language," said Panchurin, "its glory, its beauty, the ease of learning it, its antiquity, its universality, the fact that the two greatest novelists of all ages, Tolstoy and Dostoyevsky, wrote in it, and that the immortal Lenin used it to expound Marxism. But I am sure that other speakers will use much the same arguments for their own tongues, so I will refrain. You may rest assured, however, that we Russians will uphold our own glorious speech. And we are confident that many among you non-Russians also appreciate its superiority."

Scone then recognized Emile Lorilleux, the geochemist. He spoke passionately and poetically for two minutes on the beauty, the conciseness and exactness, the great adaptability, the long recognized distinction of French as a diplomatic tool, and the greatness of its literature, second to none.

There were others. Kreooson, the only Greek on the Moon, spoke even more eloquently of the unbroken continuity of his native speech, of the richness and beauty, the tongue of Homer, Euripides, Plato, Aristotle, and Kazantzakis, of the many contributions it had made and was still making to scientific and poetic discourse. Near the end, he began to look desperate, and tears appeared in his eyes.

It was then that Old Man Dahlquist asked for the floor. When he rose, there was a respectful silence and concentrated attention. Arne Dahlquist was a legend, loved by many and honored even by the Chinese. He was 90 years old, though he looked no more than sixty. He was reputed to be the greatest linguist that had ever lived; he could speak fluently every major Indo-European and Ural-Altaic language and many of the lesser. He was conversant in the Kadai-Malayo-Polynesian tongues. He talked well in Japanese, Mandarin, Cantonese, Malayalam, and Burmese, and he could talk at ease with any speaker of Navaho, Apache, Dakota, Ojibway, Cherokee, Nahuatl, Maya, or Quechua.

"As you know," he said, smiling at them. "I have been on the Moon for six years. My project was concerned with the Earth, not this satellite, and its intention was to demonstrate the single source of most of the American Indian tongues and to illustrate the relationship of the Amerindian Ursprache to Ainu. Perhaps, even to other tongues of the Old World. I came here because my project was to take a long time, and there was a greater chance of extending my life span if I lived in the less taxing gravity of the Moon.

"I brought several thousands of microfilms of my research material. This has been fortunate for future Lunarian research. Without these records, our descendants might not know anything of the great variety of tongues used on Earth, since the majority of their speakers have died. And it is probable that the bomb attack itself, plus the havoc necessarily created by Nature during the next two hundred years, will destroy most of mankind's books and records.

"'Well, that is neither here nor there, so where could it be, then?' He paused to smile at his little joke, then continued, "You have more important things to think about than linguistic scholarship, and most of you care little about such things as the structure of Nahuatl or the beauty of its literature.

"Just as your sons and daughters and their children will care little that their parents' speech is not the one they are using. All, Russian, English, Chinese, and the other nationalities represented here, will be speaking one tongue. For a while, anyway. Eventually, the speech of each base will begin to deviate into dialects. And, after Moonman has moved back to earth and established various colonies there, the dialects will evolve into separate languages. This is inevitable, but it has no bearing on the immediate future.

"What I am trying to point out to you—forgive the ramblings of an old man speaking on the subject dearest to his heart—is that there is no necessity of voting at this time on what language should be universal after peace comes—if it comes. If we come to blows with the Spanish speakers of Mars or their Bantu allies, we may be exterminated or else enslaved. In either case, our languages will no longer be a matter of choice. Our masters will impose their speech upon us. But we may win. Who knows? Only God—I use the term in a consciously mythological or literary sense only, of course —only God knows.

"But what if Martian and Moonman avoid each other, leaving each to his own destiny, thus making sure that we don't annihilate one another and put an end to mankind forever? This is a possible solution. What, then, if this state of actionless war, of eternal emergency, is maintained? Then, since English is the means of intercommunication, since it is the language with the most prestige, it will be used more and more. The other tongues will die of disuse. And they will die quickly.

"Remember, the situation is not the same here as it was on Earth. There, even a secondary tongue had many speakers to hand it on to the children. Breton and Basque took a long time a-dying, though their fate was as certain as that of Atinu or Wend or Yuma. But there are very few people on the Moon. Three hundred by latest count. If the state of war continues for a generation, a good percentage of you, as old men and women, will barely remember the tongue you now speak so trippingly.

"Therefore, I propose that we forget all about the vote. You have already decided the issue. Or, I should say Colonel Scone has done so."

He sat down, and there was a silence.

Scone did not wait for Dahlquist's words to take effect but said immediately, "The motion has been made and seconded that, after the war with the Axis is ended, we adopt one language as the primary speech for the Moon bases. Now, we don't have voting machines, so we will have to have a show of hands. To insure there's no complaint about a possible miscount, each of the bases may select one member for a hand-counting committee."

The committee was quickly chosen, and the three went up to the platform where they could have a better view. Scone then said, "All those voting yea for the motion will signify by raising hands."

Broward looked around and saw that practically the only ones holding up their hands were the native English-speakers of Clavius, a few West Europeans, an Armenian in the Russian delegation, and a Thai in the Chinese group.

Suddenly, it struck him that he had been thinking like those others who had pled for their own tongue. He had taken it for granted that the motion would be carried—because of Scone's strong action in repressing Ying—and had thought that the issue would be only which language would be selected. Now, he saw that Scone, in asking Broward to make the motion, had not told him everything. Scone might be big and impassive, but he was not unintelligent. He had, surely had, arranged with Dahlquist before the meeting to make that speech. And Dahlquist's words had had the intended effect. They had frightened everybody into wanting to put off the issue as long as possible. So, although Dahlquist had told them the truth when he said that it was not necessary to vote, he had also scared them into avoiding the issue. They thought that if they waited until peace came, then they could deal with Scone, refuse to accept one and only one language, save their beloved language for their children and grandchildren.

Only, they had either forgotten, or did not really understand, or else did not want to believe Dahlquist when he said that it was not necessary to vote.

Scone rapped his gavel and said, "Obviously, we won't have to count the nay-sayers. Very well, then. We will wait until peace comes."

Later, the others would get to thinking about what had happened and would see what Broward knew. But there would be nothing to do about it then. And, indeed, if Scone kept them busy enough, they might not have time to meditate and thus arrive at the truth.

"The next big issue is something that has to be decided at once," said Scone. "Putting it off will cause a great deal of trouble. Perhaps enough to disrupt us, make us weak for the conflict with the Axis. That problem is the shortage of women."

He paused, as if reviewing again what he must have gone over many times in his mind. It was then that a light on a squawkbox on the desk before him began flashing. He flipped a switch and leaned over close to it.

He spoke a few words, then straightened and said, "'You will have to excuse me for a few minutes. The meeting is adjourned until I return. In the meantime, be thinking about solutions to the next issue."

He stepped down off the platform and strode down the central aisle towards the exit. On reaching the first row, however, he beckoned to Broward. Broward followed him, wondering what could be important enough to call him from the meeting. Or was this move another trick by Scone? It was then that he saw Ingrid Nashdoi on a chair in the back row. He raised his eyebrows and smiled when he was sure that she saw him. She smiled back and shrugged her shoulders.

Outside the conference room, Scone said, "I just got a flash from the radar chief. Come with me to my office."

Broward followed him in. Scone sat down behind his desk and said, "A scoutship, one of our robots, finally reported in. It was one of three. I sent one; and there was a Russian and Chinese ship, also. All three were to find out what the situation on Mars is. All but ours must have been caught; anyway, they're overdue in their reports. The *Silverfish* was able to take some pretty good pictures."

He made a steeple of his hands and looked straight ahead, through Broward. Broward fidgeted a while, then said, finally, "Is it that bad?"

"Oh? Bad? Bad enough. Our Martian bases were really clobbered, though they didn't go out without a fight. One of the South African bases was destroyed; on the surface, at least. And there's evidence that Deimos was hit. So badly, in fact, that the garrison didn't respond to the scout's presence. It made no effort to fire; it didn't even emit any radar or lasers, none that the scout detected."

"So the Martian Axe is a definite threat?"

"More than that. The scout also detected an immense fleet moving towards Mars, approximately ten million miles away from it."

"It couldn't be ours," said Broward. "It would have come here first."

"Undoubtedly, it's the Argentinean main fleet, carrying Felipe Howards. Probably, the aristocracy of the Axe Party and their families, too. Do you see what this means?"

Broward shook his head, and Scone continued. "It means that Howards planned to set off those cobalt bombs. He intended to destroy all life on Earth and then rebuild a new society, an all-Axe world. It'll be started on Mars, and, when Earth is ready for resettling, completed on Earth. A totally Spanish-speaking fascist world."

"He'd have to be a raving maniac to do that!" said Broward.

"He's a maniac all right, but he knows what he's doing and how to do it," said Scone. "The thing is, he hasn't finished his job. He must know by now that his forces failed on the Moon, and he'll want to make sure of the Soviet bases on Ganymede and Mercury, too. So, we can expect some action in the near future. The hell of it is, if that fleet is as big as the scout reported, Howards has the muscle to beat us. He could lose half his fleeet and still have twice as many ships and missiles as we can muster. Plus the fact that his forces are unified. They don't have to guard against each other while they're fighting the enemy."

"You didn't call me in here just to tell me this."

"Of course not. Bob, I have something special I want you to do."

Broward knew then that Scone was planning something of utmost importance and extreme danger. This was the first time that he had ever called him by his first name. But there must be even more than that to cause him to do so. Could it be that what Scone wanted him to do was so dangerous that even he hesitated to ask? Or was it something else, something sinister in Scone's motive?

"The point is this," said Scone. "We are badly outnumbered and outweaponed. The Martians have every advantage over us, aside, of course, from operating on the basis of an incorrect ideology. But I have never noticed that being ideologically perverted kept any nation from being excellent fighters. I can say this in the privacy of my office; I know that you would not think of repeating it."

"You said that the point is . . . ?"

"If the Martians bring their full weight against us, and I see no reason why they won't, we'll be wiped out. So, we can strip the bases of all that the ships can carry and find a hiding place, a new colony. We might even all board the *Zemlya* and take off for the stars, leaving the Axis in full possession of the solar system.

"I don't like to do that; in fact, I won't.

"Two, we can beat the Martians to the punch. But there is only one way to do that. Somebody must go to Earth and get the means to enable us to smash the Martians. More than that. Smash Mars!"

"I don't understand," said Broward.

"Planetbuster," said Scone. "Did you ever hear of it?"

"No."

"It is—was—top secret, but that, of course doesn't mean that word somehow wouldn't get around. The Russians were building it. It was, if my intelligence is right, a device 100% efficient in converting matter into energy. And it was supposed to have an amplification factor in it. You might say it was 500% efficient. Yes, I know, that's impossible. But, effectively that was what it was supposed to do. Don't ask me the principle behind it.

"This—call it a bomb—was not intended to be used as a weapon on Earth. It would have destroyed the Russians also, even if set off at the South Pole. But the Russians wanted to build and test one. They had planned to explode it on Juno. It was their prediction that the asteroid, even though it has a diameter of 210 kilometers, would be shattered into a million tiny fragments."

Broward felt frozen. He said, "You can't be thinking of sending some one down there . . . ?"

"Why not?" replied Scone. "I'd go myself, but it's obvious that I must stay here. I know where the bomb is located. And we have a small experimental vessel that's shielded heavily enough to withstand twenty times the radiation you'll find down there. Moreover, I've already given orders to have special suits equipped for any work you have to do outside the ship. Believe me, it can be done. I've talked to those who know, and they've told me it can be done."

"But, even if it's found, how do you know it'll be operative? Who knows how to control it?"

Broward became aware that he was breathing hard and that his fists were clenched.

"Why me?" he said, "I'm a physical anthropologist and a doctor! What do I know about getting a ship down there, or handling a device of that nature?"

"You're a doctor, and you've had a great deal of training in radiation. You won't be piloting the ship; another man will do that. As for the bomb, it's a comparatively small package, and perfectly safe. Besides, I picked you for another reason I haven't mentioned yet."

"What's that?" said Broward. He caught himself in time, bit down on the words. A little more anger, and he would have accused Scone of sending him in order to have a free hand with Ingrid.

"Didn't you spend a year in East Siberia on an anthropological study of the descendants of the colonists?"

"Yes," said Broward. "What of it?"

"The bomb is located in an underwater installation off the coast of East Siberia."

Broward sighed. Trust the man to have checked through the biographical files to find data he could use. Scone had him. He was, in many ways, a logical choice.

"Am I being ordered to go? Or being asked to volunteer?" he said.

"The survival of all men on the Moon demands that someone get that bomb. You should be proud because I think enough of your qualifications to order you to go."

Broward knew better than to ask him what would happen if he refused. For a moment, he wondered if Scone wanted him to rebel. That would give Scone an easy and legal way to get rid of Broward. Now, there was a chance Broward could return from the mission. How much chance, Broward would not know until he evaluated the situation.

"Who's going with me?" he said.

"Captain Yamanuchi will be your pilot and navigator."

"You think of everything," Broward said.

Fleetingly, Scone looked surprised. But if he guessed what Broward meant, he did not care to pursue it.

"It'll be some time before the ship is ready," Scone said. "Report to Dr. Wellers in Section T. I'll see you before you leave."

"Yes, sir," Broward answered. He saluted, spun around, and walked stiffly out of the office. His only thought was to talk to Ingrid before he left. He did not care what obstacles Scone would put in his way to prevent that.

Wellers and Yamanuchi were waiting for him. Wellers was a tall thin Englishman with large brown eyes and sunken cheeks. He had two Ph.D.'s, one in selenic physics, one in spatial navigation. Generally, he was regarded as a nut. His outspokenness had gotten him in trouble, but he was so brilliant that the Terrestrial authorities had ignored his views as much as possible. They had sent him to the Moon where he would have only a small audience and could be watched more closely. His case, however, was nothing unusual. The Moon was half-populated with people of dubious views but great usefulness.

The other man was Moshe Yamanuchi. He was stocky, about thirty, had light-brown curly hair and deep purple-blue eyes with long eyelashes. Aside from his name, he had nothing about him to indicate his Japanese ancestry. In his own way, he was even more of a curiosity than Wellers. His grandfather, one of the many Japanese converted to Judaism some time after World War II, had emigrated to Israel. He had married a Sabra of Danish-Polish-Scotch descent. The second son of this union had taken to wife a woman of Dutch-Czech-Algerian ancestry. Moshe, their last child, was born in northern Alaska; his parents had been among the victims of the Third Diaspora, moved by the Soviets in their effort to demolish forever the Israeli state and Judaism.

Moshe Yamanuchi was the only "Jew" on the Moon. It was said that Moshe had been assigned there by mistake. He was not listed as having a religion and he had applied for membership to the Communist Party. The officials who had sent him to the Moon had been misled by his surname, and so on. When it finally became known, and Scone was notified that a man of Jewish "blood" was under his command, nothing was done about it. Yamanuchi was a likeable and valuable man, and people found it difficult to believe that he could actually be a Jew. He didn't fit the picture.

Moshe himself, though he claimed to be an atheist, joked about his divinity. He was both the son of David and the Sun-goddess. The blood of Solomon and Abraham and the Mikados flowed in a duke's mixture through his veins, he said, although it flowed somewhat sluggishly, since it was also cold Alaskan blood.

Now, looking at Yamanuchi, Broward thought of Scone's motives for sending this man with him. He was as good as any for a job like this, better than most. Yet, if he did not return, he would be a victim of Scone's "killing two birds with one stone" policy. Scone would have rid himself of the "Japanese Jew."

The two men greeted Broward. Wellers began at once to give them information by lecture and by the scope pictures on the console. Photographs, diagrams, mathematical equations, lines of text appeared on the large screen. Wellers explained in a high-pitched monotonous voice. Two hours later, the two soldiers knew thoroughly the essential details. The vital mathematical facts involving the navigational problems were already taped and checked and on the way to the ship.

"Both the ship and your mobile suits will be extra-protected from the high radiation by the misnamed anti-fields," said Wellers. "You'll be safe—as long as the field generators work. They have been known to malfunction at critical occasions."

"It's like getting a pep talk from Father Death himself," Yamanuchi said.

"I wish I could be with you," Wellers replied. "You'll be getting a direct observation of what's happened to Earth."

Broward shuddered and said, "'If I had my way, you could take my place."

The IP shrilled. "Captain Broward! Report at once to Section G."

Broward went to the IP. "Broward speaking. Any idea why I'm wanted in G?"

"This is Eilers, Sperm Bank. We want a deposit, Captain. Scone's orders."

Broward said, "Received. Be there in a minute." Then, as an afterthought, "What about Captain Yamanuchi."

"I've got no orders about him."

"Has he already made a deposit?"

"Young and Yexa are the only ones in the Y file. Why?"

"Nothing," said Broward.

He was sick. Yamanuchi, the handsome, intelligent, and tough one, was to be denied a chance to contribute to the betterment of the human species. Scone did not want "tainted" genes.

"Don't look so stricken," Moshe said. He was smiling. "I know exactly why I'm not being asked to commit the sin of Onan. But Scone's dealing with a very tricky Jew. I've already taken the necessary steps—horizontally, that is, if you can take steps horizontally—to ensure that I have at least two children. Maybe more, since twins run in my family."

Broward grinned and said, "Do I understand. . . ? Why, you philandering barnyard rooster, you!"

"If there is one trait I have inherited from my remote ancestor, King David, it is a powerful hunger for beautiful women and the ability to, pardon the expression, draw them like flies to honey. There are two lovely females—discretion and an old-fashioned sense of honor seal my lips concerning their names—who at this moment are nourishing the fruits of our loves in their wombs.

"In death-time, a young man's fancy turns to thoughts

of love. In other words, when I considered that my line, my species, might become extinct unless I did my duty, I seed my duty and I done it, no pun intended it. Although I must admit I enjoyed it, and I don't mean the pun."

"If Scone hears of this," Broward said, "he'll have you shot. You know what a stiff-necked moralist he is, when it comes to sex, anyway."

"While others dawdle, I delve," Moshe replied. "And he won't hear of it. Not unless . . ."

Wellers said, "I didn't hear a thing. I wouldn't want to start an investigation of that sort. The hunters might start sniffing around my lair and unearth the fact that I sometimes mix a high-minded concern for mathematics with an interest in things they might consider low-minded."

The two soldiers laughed and walked from the lab. Outside Broward said, "Something puzzles me. You said you wouldn't commit the sin of Onan even if ordered to. Why not? An orthodox Hebrew might object to giving his sperm to the bank, but you. . . ?"

"We'll talk about that later," Moshe replied. "During the trip out."

Suddenly, he lost his gayety; his face was grave.

They walked silently down the corridors hewn out of basalt. Just before they parted at a junction, Moshe rubbed his chin. In a low tone, as if talking to himself or some third party, he said, "All right. I'll grow a beard."

"What?" Broward exclaimed, but Moshe was walking away.

A moment later, Broward heard his name over the IP. It was followed by an announcement that the takeoff was delayed. There was a malfunction in the anti-radiation field generator. His scalp felt icy; he remembered Wellers' comment about this possibility.

After promising to check in from time to time, Broward walked towards the conference room. He passed through silent hall after hall, his way lit before him by bright luminescent panels which sprang into glow as he neared them. Before him was blackness and after him was blackness. He was enveloped by a moving halo. Was this, he thought, the plight of the human being? Unable to see the past and the future, only capable of viewing his immediate time and location. True, he knew where he had been and thought he knew where he was going. But, if the lights failed, could he go towards his destination without taking the wrong turn?

Under his feet, the rock trembled as the borers far under drove in their quest for water. What if their goal turned out to be a deposit of some combination of explosive chemicals? The blast could conceivably wreck the base and kill every one on it. Then what? There would be a few men and women left on the Russian and Chinese bases and a few in the Ganymedan and Mercutian bases (if these still existed). The people of Mars (the enemies) would determine the future of mankind (if the Martians had not been exterminated). It was true that the large Axe fleet was moving towards Mars. But the ships might contain very few women.

What if Nature or God or Whoever decided that mankind was so few in numbers he was now below the survival level? And, in the so far inscrutable ways of the universe, the women left would just cease to bear? Consider those species that had in the past been reduced to near-extinction on Earth. A few females still lived, theoretically capable of reproducing and of starting anew the species. But, for some reason, they could not have young. Nature had called a halt; she had turned her back on the species.

If this should happen to us, thought Broward, we deserve it. Man, the Mad Thinker, the Irrational Rationalist, the Illogical Logician who thought himself into oblivion.

"The next thing you know," he muttered to himself, "I'll be believing in God." And he considered how the loneliness and the darkness had thrust him so swiftly into the mental condition of the frightened savage.

Then, he was in the well-lighted hall leading to the conference room, and Ingrid Nashdoi was coming through the door towards him. She looked furious, and she started to walk by him. But he reached out and seized her arm.

"What's the matter?"

"Take your hands off me!" she cried. "You . . . you *man!*"

"All right," he said gently. "What's my gender done to yours?"

Tears streamed down her cheeks. "They just decided that it's only fair . . . for the men, of course, never mind us . . . oh, those men . . ."

"You're incoherent," he said. "And all the time I thought you were Ingrid."

"Jokes! Jokes at a time like this! Can't you see I'm crying?"

"I'm just trying to calm you down."

She put her head on his shoulder. His arms went around

her, and her shoulders began to shake while her tears wet his uniform.

"They've decided . . . to make every woman be the mate of two or more men . . . or whatever the proportion of men to women might be! It's for the good of humanity . . . they say. And there were women who voted along with the men for it! Women!"

"Did Scone push that through?" said Broward. "That . . ."

Ingrid stepped back from his arms and looked up at him. "Oh, no, I'll say that for him. He fought it. He said we shouldn't do anything about the man-woman ratio until we'd settled the account with Mars. For once, he couldn't get his way. He was shouted down. Those men were like a pack of howling wolves."

"Sure, he opposed it. He wants you for himself."

Ingrid took a handkerchief from her coverall pocket and dabbed at her eyes. "Well, he can't have me. At least, I'll be able to pick the men I want. You can bet your bottom ruble that he won't be one of them. Unless he's one of those left over after all the picking and choosing is done. Then, he'll be assigned by a committee. And the poor woman that gets him won't have a thing to say about it."

Broward said, "I suppose that, the situation being what it is, nothing else could be done. It's . . ."

"What kind of a man are you?" she wailed, and she began crying again.

"I'm trying to be logical. Objective. Getting emotional isn't going to help any."

"Well, I intend to be emotional. All emotional. I haven't got a bit of logic about this, and I don't intend to have any! Are you really telling me you'll stand by while some other man takes me off to bed?"

"If there's a way out, I'll think of it," he said. "But it'll take brain power, not tears."

Ingrid turned away from him and ran away. He watched her flight down the hall, the luminescence of the panels keeping pace with her. "A firefly," he thought. "In reverse. The flames pursuing her."

And he laughed, though weakly, at himself. Always the romantic poet, no matter what the situation.

He decided it would do no good at the moment to follow her and try to comfort her. He entered the conference room in time to hear Scone appoint a committee of nine. This was to consider methods for implementing the new rule, already termed "Sexual Grouping Policy" After drawing up a set of principles and rules for enforcing them, the committee was to submit them for a general vote.

Some of the women were angry, and some were pale with shock. But it was obvious that nothing could have more pleased Sonya Abarbanel, the beautiful biochemist. Seeing her, Broward became even more angry. For a second, he thought of proposing that the problem be solved by making her an official whore for both Eratosthenes and Clavius. Then, controlling himself, he saw how ridiculous he would appear and what a sharp public rebuke he would receive.

Nevertheless, he could not help loathing her. It did not detract from his feeling to remind himself that he had once had an affair with her. His celibate life on the Moon had made him an easy prey for her—if prey was the word for such a willing participant as himself. Then, on discovering that she was bedding with at least ten other men at the same time, he had quit her in disgust and shame.

A moment later, as usual, he regretted his loathing. Poor creature, she could not help it. Who knew what strange and powerful desires moved her, what her compulsions were? And she had served—was serving—a deep need. Many of the men led monastic lives here. As long as they were to be here only a year or two, they could be supposed to endure the enforced continence or could not be blamed if they took advantage of any chance to break it.

But, no man now could be expected to live like a holy hermit the rest of his life, especially since, unlike the ancient hermit, he would come into daily contact with women. So, despite his anger and Ingrid's grief, he had to admit that the decision was the only one to make. That did not mean he had to like it.

It was a mess, and God only knew how many heartbreaks—his among them—would result.

His attention was caught by the man then speaking from the floor. He was Pierre Schwartz, the only Swiss on the Moon, and he was making a motion that nationalism be condemned. He proposed that each base transfer a third of its personnel to another. This would also pave the way for men to think of themselves as Soviets only, not American Soviets or Russian or Chinese Soviets. It would be a foolproof way to make certain that their sons and daughters would think of themselves as members of a single group.

Several dozen people leaped up, shaking their fists and

screaming at Schwartz. Order was restored only by Scone's gavel and his roaring.

"Schwartz! I am denying you the right to make such a motion! You yourself are the living proof that people of different national origins and speaking different languages can live harmoniously! You are—were—a citizen of Switzerland! Sit down, or I shall expel you from the meeting!"

Shrugging, the Swiss obeyed. Immediately, Jack Campbell, a Canadian, got Scone's recognition.

"Mr. Chairman, are we to understand that the principle of nationalism—although basically not one of Marx's tenets—is the recognized rule on the Moon? And, when we return to Earth, on Earth?"

"It is, Mr. Campbell."

"I have just been talking to Mr. Gomez, a Mexican, and Mr. Lorilleux, a Frenchman. We agree that, following your rule, we each have a valid right to a base where we may establish and preserve our own nationalities. Contrary to what you seem to take for granted, those of us who are not Yankees are not happy at the prospect of becoming Yankees. We are as proud of our nationalities as you are of yours."

For the first time since Broward had known him, Scone became red in the face.

He shouted, "It's obvious to anyone but an idiot that this rule can be followed only when practical! We don't have the means for every piddling little national to go his own way. What would you do, have us dig you two cells in the rock a thousand miles away and set a dome over it and hoist the Canadian flag over it? And do the same for the Swiss, and the Frenchman, and the Mexican, and the Swede? How would you reproduce? Would each of you take a woman with you, a woman who probably would not want to give up her nationality for yours?

"No, Mr. Campbell, you're being utterly ridiculous. You know it; you're trying to wreck the proceedings of this conference, and trying to make me look foolish."

"If I'm ridiculous," said Campbell, "then so is everyone else here, you included. There aren't more than three hundred people on the Moon, yet you talk of maintaining nationalities and separate bases. We need each other. We must tear down all barriers. I think that Schwartz's proposal is a very sensible one, the only one, in fact. Unless we all move into one base."

Broward was about to leap to his feet to back Campbell

when he became aware of a man standing by him. He looked up to see Sergeant Ross.

"Time for you to report to the *Dorland*, sir."

Broward started to ask why an escort had been sent for him. Then, he closed his mouth. Scone did not want him to talk to Ingrid before he left.

He rose and said, "I want to see somebody for a minute."

The sergeant looked at his watch and shook his head. "No time, sir. Your takeoff is automatic; your flight path is, too, until you reach your destination. You can't be one second behind time."

Broward knew that this was not true. The latest navigational equipment had capabilities for self-adjustment to changes. But Scone must have given Ross strict orders. Sighing, Broward nodded and walked out of the room.

He found Moshe and Wellers and several engineers and technicians waiting for him. Wellers gave them final instructions. Then, just as they were ready to board the *Dorland*, they saw a sergeant enter. He held a carton of cigarettes in his hand.

Coming up to Broward, he saluted, then said, "Compliments of Colonel Scone, sir."

Broward took the carton and said, "That's very nice of the colonel, Sergeant. Tell him thanks for me."

"It's the last one in Clavius, sir," replied the sergeant. "Maybe the last in the whole Moon."

"And he sent it to me," murmured Broward.

"In the old days, the condemned were always given a big meal and cigarettes just before the execution," Yamanuchi said.

Yes, thought Broward, but this gift was not one to be expected from Scone. He was thoroughly unsentimental. Moreover, Scone smoked and giving this carton meant a sacrifice for him. Until the tobacco plants were taken from the *Zemlya's* tanks and placed in a garden in the Moon, there would be no more smokes for the Moon personnel. And it was not likely that it would be grown for a long time. The strict economy of the Moon could not afford the luxury of tobacco fields.

Maybe, thought Broward, it would be better if the plant was never taken out of the tanks. Most of mankind had gotten along quite well without nicotine before Columbus, and they'd be much better off without it now.

Be that as it might, Scone's act was entirely unexpected.

"You smoke?" he said to the sergeant.

"Not for long," the sergeant replied. "I got half a pack left, and I'm nursing that."

"Here," said Broward, handing the carton to him, "take a couple of packs. Pass the rest around among your men."

Broward raised his hand to stop the sergeant's protests. "I have to quit sometime; I may not live long enough to get through a pack. No use wasting them."

He turned away and said, "Let's go, Moshe."

They entered the ship through an airlock and seated themselves in two chairs placed just before the control panel and observation screen. The sergeant pressed a button on the panel; long slender rods topped by curved metal plates rose from orifices in the chairs and clamped themselves around the heads, chests, arms, and legs of the two seated men. The sergeant then pressed another button; nothing seemed to result from the action. But the sergeant, testing, found that he could not push his hand through the "stasis" field that now surrounded the two. He signalled to them, and both depressed a plate on the right arm of their chairs. Immediately, the sergeant could extend his hand as near them as he wished.

"The stasis is O.K.," he said. "Reactivate it now."

Broward and Yamanuchi settled back. The plates on the rods were not restraining devices but reminders that they must stay in the chair. One of the peculiarities of the not well-understood stasis was that a material object on the outside of the field could not pass through, not unless it was hurled with much more energy than the muscles of a man could expend. Light and sound could pass through the stasis both ways, and a man within it could easily walk out through it. If, however, during the state of terrific acceleration that would be experienced by the ship on most of its journey to the Earth, a man within stasis were to stick so much as a finger through the field, he would be sucked out into the "normal" fields and would be subject to them. That is, he would be crushed to death.

The sergeant made some rechecks of equipment, saluted the two, and left. They, looking at the energized screen, saw only the seeming flat plain of the floor of Clavius, cleared of moondust, the near horizon, Earth hanging close to the horizon, and the hard glare of the stars. Then, so swiftly that they could not at once comprehend it, even though they were expecting and had experienced the sensation, they were away from the moon and in the glare of the sun. Before them, on the control panel, the red light in the G column crept upwards; they were already past fifty gravities.

The round of the Earth, dark on their left, luminous on their right, perceptibly ballooned. Outlines of the continents and the flashings of the sun from the oceans and big lakes were missing. Since that fatal day, the Earth had been covered with clouds. Even the ice caps of the Poles were smudged.

The two men were silent for a long time. Broward found himself reaching towards his pocket for a cigarette. He smiled, but he wondered if he had not been too impulsive in giving away all his tobacco. Not that he could smoke now, anyway. Light and sound and air could travel through the barrier. Theoretically, it was safe to smoke, but regulations forbade.

Broward turned his head to look at Moshe on his left. Moshe had his eyes closed, and he was smiling slightly.

"Thinking of women again?" said Broward.

"Bagels and lox," said Moshe. "Sara Bagels and Judith Lox, that is."

Moshe laughed, then said, "I'm lying. I was thinking of my mother and father."

"And you can laugh?"

"Laughter and tears are means of relieving tension. Sometimes, I laugh when others cry, and vice versa. Maybe it's because I've had to dissimulate all my life. It's not easy to be a Jew."

"You're not a Jew," said Broward.

"Tell the others that. Tell them that being a Jew is a matter of one's *religion*, not of one's genes or whatever faith one's parents happened to be."

"That's all in the past," said Broward. "People will forget after a while. Even if there is some slight feeling left in their relations with you, your children won't be affected by it."

"My parents made an effort to educate me in their religion. Secretly, of course. Nominally, they were atheists, but they celebrated all the old ceremonies: Passover, Rosh Hashanah, and so on. They even gave me a Bar Mitzvah; there were twelve others present then, all masked, of course, so nobody would know who they were. Although I was the only one who didn't know. Maybe they were afraid I'd turn them in. Rightly so. Not that I did or even thought of doing so for a moment. I mean they were right not to take the chance that I would.

"But I went through the ceremony only to please them, I had no interest whatsoever or belief in perpetuating their faith. I just wanted to forget about the whole ridiculous and tragic thing."

He was silent for a moment, then said, as if continuing aloud his thought and as if not addressing Broward, "But I can't forget. It's not that a voice has spoken to me out of the fire in the bushes. But there's a voice. Or a reasonable facsimile thereof."

"You're letting the events of the last two weeks get to you," said Broward. "The old world is destroyed, and there's nothing you can do about it. But we do have a new world to make, and if we profit by the mistakes the old world made, we'll . . ."

"You have as much chance getting everybody to agree on what the brave new world should be as Scone will have on getting everybody to agree to make the Moon a New America," said Moshe.

Broward did not reply. It was true that Moshe was a member of his Athenian party, but Broward had all along felt that Moshe had joined him only in protest against the Communists. He did not have a sincere or deep belief in the principles Broward expounded. Not in the ability of men to carry out the principles, anyway. When Moshe had lost his faith in the God of his fathers—if he ever had any—he had also lost his faith in men.

The rest of the way the two talked about trivial things, about those they knew on the Moon, about friends and enemies they had known on Earth, their childhoods, jokes. Exactly one and a half hours after they had hurtled from the surface of the Moon, an alarm rang through the ship. This, as the appropriate blinking light on the panel validated, was the signal that the ship was beginning to decelerate. It was not needed, for the vessel had been on automatic from the beginning. It would continue to be so until it had brought them into the atmosphere and close to the area where they were to land. Then, Moshe would take over the controls.

They waited, silently, while the ship plunged into the clouds that blanketed the planet. Broward showed his nervousness by the swift tapping of his fingers on the chair-arm; Moshe hummed softly. Outside, all was gloom except for flashes of lightning in the distance. Suddenly, they were in a heavy rain.

"We're on the nightside," said Moshe. "Out of contact

with the Moon. There's nothing to keep us from taking off
again, keeping the Earth between us and the Moon until we
are out of detection range."

"Where would we go?" said Broward. "And why should
we go?"

"Ganymede. Mercury. Ganymede'd be better. Did you
ever read the report on the complex of caverns in it? A whole
city could hide there and never be found. As to why, well,
why go back to a people that hate you or, at least, have
contempt for you? Or to a leader that wants to use you as
tools for his own twisted ideology, not as a human being with
rights and desires of his own? And . . ."

"We have to stick together to survive," said Broward.
"Centripetal force is what we need, not centrifugal desires
that will whirl us apart."

"Forget it. I'm just talking. First, let's find what we came
for, then . . ."

Their goal was ten kilometers off the coast of the East
Siberian Sea, near the city of Yakan, and a quarter of a
kilometer beneath the surface. The ship took them to the exact
spot—or so the instruments indicated—and then it poised
ten meters above the waves. So thick was the mixture of
smoke and fog, that the two men could see nothing. They
had not glimpsed the land once during their descent. Broward
had wanted to see something of the devastation. At the same
time, he did not want to see it. He was not sure that he could
bear the sight. Knowing about it had been almost too much;
to view the glassed-over and fused cities that had suffered
direct hits, to see the shattered remnants of the areas that
had been on the fringes, to have to see the thousands, the
millions of bodies of those who had died from radiation, the
human beings, the animals, birds . . . this was more than he
could endure even to imagine. No, he was glad that the
smoke from burning cities and the forests hid dead Earth.

He pressed the button that released them from stasis, rose,
and went to the control panel. Powerful searchlights stabbed
into the brown-grey mists. Below, the huge waves of the sea
raced up and down. Then, they were near, lashing at the ship;
then, the waves were gone, and the darkness of the sea,
speared by the light beams, was around them. There were no
fish to be startled by the frightening appearance of the strong
lights.

Abruptly, one of the rays struck a projection, obviously not
a natural formatin. It reared 200 meters above the black

ooze of the sea bottom. Moshe guided the vessel above the flat top of the tower, halted it above the exact center, and pressed another button.

"According to what Ziolsky told Scone, the port is set to activate only to a certain sonar code. Ziolsky was not sure the code would not be changed by now. But, if the code doesn't work, we can enter by another port, near the base, in our suits."

"It's working," said Moshe, pointing at the door sinking within the flat surface of the tower top. He lowered the ship past the entrance. The ponderous door stopped retreating directly in front of them and began to slide to one side within the inner wall of the great tube. The vessel dropped below it. Broward, looking at a screen which gave a view of the exterior from above, saw the door move ponderously but swiftly from the wall, then begin to move upwards, to reseal the opening.

The ship was stopped from further descent by a metal floor, but around them, piercing the walls, were four openings each large enough to admit a vessel twice the size of theirs. Moshe chose the one straight ahead of him; the forward beams showed them that the tunnel dipped sharply downwards. They followed this decline for perhaps 350 meters, then were floating on the surface of the water, and they were in a blaze of lights.

"Here's where we get out," said Moshe. He lifted the ship from the water and deposited it on the other side of one of the dozen docking berths. All of these were occupied by a vessel. Broward checked the radiation meter and found what he had expected. A background normal for this level.

"Do you suppose that there could still be people living down here?" he said.

"Why not?" replied Moshe. "If what you told me was valid, there were quite a few personnel here. The question is, did they stay here?"

A few minutes later, they left the ship. They were clad in coveralls and carried only automatics as weapons and a small gravity-propelled blaster for drilling in case they encountered any doors that refused to open to normal means. Near the entrance to a tunnel leading inwards was a small car, a Siberian *Voluto*. It was ready to go, so the two climbed in with Moshe at the controls. He found that it could not be lifted more than seven centimeters off the floor; evidently, it had a governor on the motor. He began to drive it down the tunnel, which was identified by Arabic numerals and Cyrillic characters. Broward, comparing these against the map given him by Scone, quickly found where they were and where they were going. At the first junction they came to, he directed Moshe to take the tunnel to the extreme left. Moshe obeyed, and they shot down it at top speed, 20 kilometers per hour. On either side of the tunnel were doors, all shut.

"I'd say everybody had left if it weren't for those ships in the dock," said Moshe. "So, where is everybody?"

"Mass suicide?" said Broward. "Not likely. There'd be a few that would live as long as they could draw a breath."

Moshe shouted and stabbed his finger at a button and the little car stopped. Ahead of them, a plate of plastic had dropped down and completely blocked the tunnel. And the rear view mirror showed that the same thing had happened behind them.

"Good thing we brought the driller," said Moshe. He started to climb out of the car but stopped when a voice blared at them.

"Drop your weapons on the floor. Go to the shield nearest you; face it; raise your hands in the air. Remain immobile until you are told otherwise!"

The voice, coming from a loudspeaker located somewhere in the wall, spoke in the East Siberian Russian dialect. The two men loosened their belts, dropped them, and then proceeded to obey directions. No sooner had they faced the plastic wall than it rose to reveal four men on the other side. These held guns pointed at the two.

"Boris Voget!" said Moshe. "Don't you remember me, Yamanuchi?"

Voget, a tall gangling man with a Lincolnesque face, smiled and said, "Surely, it can't be the Japanese Jew? Moshe Yamanuchi! But I thought that you . . ."

"I was on the Moon," Moshe said.

"Then what are you doing here?" said Voget. His smile was gone.

"I was sent by the commander of the surviving Soviet forces on the moon," replied Moshe. "He . . ." and Moshe hesitated.

Broward guessed why he did not know what to say next. Should he tell them that his sole reason for being here was to obtain the planet-shaker, that he had thought that every living thing on Earth was dead? What if these people here did not care to place themselves under the disposition of Scone? The Siberians were famous for their desire for independence, their underground movements. The experiment conducted by the Russians in transporting enormous numbers from every place in the world to settle here had been successful in that the colonists had succeeded in making the area a fertile one. But they had brought with them an anti-Russian feeling that had not died out in their descendants.

Perhaps, thought Broward, if they knew that a North American now held the whiphand on the moon, the Siberians might be friendly. But what would they think when they discovered that their supposedly secret area was known? What would they do? Much of what would happen would depend on what Yamanuchi and Broward told them.

After being searched, the two Moonmen were conducted to a large car and made to sit in the back seats while two Siberians held guns on them. A third talked softly into a wrist-radio. A man got into the *Voluto* and followed them through the various tunnels until they reached a large room that was at least a kilometer square and 40 meters high. This had been hewed out of the rock below the sea bottom.

"They're in the same situation as we on the Moon," said Moshe to Broward. "Except that nobody knows this place is occupied by living men."

Broward could see at once what Scone would think when —and if—he found out about this place. It would offer a refuge from the danger of the Martian attack.

Near a tall tunnel entrance topped with a legend: *Chief of Operations,* the car stopped. All got out, and the two Moonmen were led into the tunnel and thence through a series of other rooms until they came to a large office. On the way, they passed at least a dozen men and women, either working at desks or on sentinel duty. The goal was a big room with a large desk. Behind it sat a thick-bodied man with very broad shoulders and a large heavily-boned head. His skin was dark; his eyes, black; his nose, an eagle's. He was dressed in coveralls and was the only person the two had so far seen who was not in uniform.

Voget, Moshe's acquaintance, had talked enough during the ride to give them a little information on the man behind the desk. He was Dr. Pyotr, the former head of the scientific operations, a physicist. His father had been a Sioux Indian, and his mother was a Saudi Arabian. The day after the war, Pyotr, in company with a band of his scientific workers and some military personnel, had arrested the commander of the project, shot several soldiers and civilians who had resisted, and taken over the leadership of the only human beings left alive in the world—as far as they knew.

Broward, looking at Pyotr, saw a man who reminded him of Scone. He had the same aura of strength and of confidence and gave the same impression of a man who would knock down and crush any one who got between him and his goal.

Pyotr's voice was as muscular as his body. He said, "I know who you are, or who you claim to be. Let's hear your story."

Broward, as nominal superior, felt he should talk. He did so without holding anything back because he expected that Pyotr would, sooner or later, find out the truth. He did not look like a man who would tolerate being lied to.

After listening to Broward's story, frequently interrupted by questions from him, Pyotr was silent for a while. Then, he said, "If I keep you here, Scone may send out another party. He wants the bomb pretty badly, and I can see why. And if we keep the second expedition, then. . . ?"

"He'll come in full force," said Broward. The bomb is his only chance of defeating the Axe."

"We can't fight him," said Pyotr. "If we sealed up the tower, he'd just blast his way in, drown us, no matter how many of his own he lost in the process. Am I right?"

"Right."

"On the other hand, if I were to destroy the bomb, he'd have no reason to bother with us. Right?"

"Wrong. If you did that, you'd be his enemy. He'd just drop a hydrogen bomb by the tower. You can't defend yourself."

"Mars is as much a threat to us as the Moon," said Pyotr. "They don't know about us now, but if they attack the Moon, which they may be doing at this moment, and crush the Moon forces . . . well, if anything is left of the bases, the Axe might find references to us in the files."

"I doubt that Scone has recorded this expedition," said Broward.

"And the Axe must not have heard about us, otherwise, we'd have heard from them long ago. They'd know as well as Scone what the bomb means."

Pyotr paused and made a steeple of his huge brown hands and rolled his eyes upward as if in prayer. Broward wondered how Pyotr would handle this. No matter which way he moved, he would be in a very bad situation. That is, unless he had some place else on Earth to hide.

Abruptly, Pyotr said to the guards, "Take them away." They were led back into the huge center room, across, and down another tunnel. The room they were locked into was a small one with two bunk beds along one wall, a chemical toilet, a small washbowl, soap, and towels. The lighting was from luminescent panels.

"We're creating consternation," said Moshe. He laughed. "God, that's the beautiful thing about life! You can't ever predict what's going to happen! Who would have thought, who could have foretold, when we left the Moon, that we'd be prisoners? And Pyotr, two hours ago, thought he was safe, ruler of all the people in the world, the little father, the Moses of the submarine world. Now, look at him. He has to save his people. At once. Right away."

Broward paced back and forth like a tiger in a narrow cage. "I wonder if Man's worth saving," he said. "He almost succeeds in annihilating himself. But, despite himself, he's given another chance. You'd think every man and woman left alive would think of only one thing, of perpetuating the species. You'd think that everybody would forget his national and ideological differences, would say to every other man, 'Let's lay down our arms, work together, make sure that we live and that our sons and daughters live and their children live, and ensure that they have a worthwhile world to live in, make sure that this doesn't happen again.' But they don't. They're all fighting each other as if nothing had happened. Is man logical but irrational? Logical in effectively carrying out his irrationalities? Is he worth saving?"

"If he survives, then he's worth it," said Moshe. "If he dies, then he's not worth it; he proved it by becoming extinct. Why worry about something abstract like that? Let's consider how we're going to get out of this."

"All right. Let's think about Pyotr. What can he do? He could detour Scone. Go to the Russians or the Chinese. But what kind of a deal could he make with them? None that would be any better than a deal with Scone. He couldn't trust them. No, the only thing for him to do is to leave his once-safe snug little nest and hide elsewhere. But where could that be?"

He stopped talking; the door had swung open. A young woman carrying a tray of food entered. Behind her were two men with guns. She was a tall well-built woman with wide shoulders, beautiful but rather strong features, green eyes, and auburn hair. She set the tray down on the lower bunk and said, "Eat, citizens, while I question you about certain matters."

Broward looked at the emblem on her uniform and said, "Psychological warfare?"

Before she could reply, Moshe said something to her in a foreign tongue which Broward identified as Hebrew, although he was not familiar enough with the language to understand it.

She looked startled, then replied swiftly in the same tongue.

The two guards looked uneasy. One said, "What are you doing, Katashkina?"

She answered in Russian, "He thinks I look like a girl he used to know. An Israeli."

The guard exploded with laughter, then said, "You, a Jew?"

The other guard said, dourly, "How do you happen to be able to talk Hebrew? That was Hebrew, wasn't it?"

"I know many languages," she said.

Moshe spoke again in Hebrew, and she answered briefly. Thereafter, the conversation was in Russian or English, but Broward detected that Moshe was elated. She asked them questions about their life on the Moon and events since the war. Several times, she required that they identify Moon personnel with detailed descriptions.

"What are you trying to do?" Broward said. "Establish that we are not Axe spies? If we'd been Axe, all we would have had to do to dispose of you was to drop a bomb on the tower."

She did not reply to him but instead continued her line of interrogation. Finally, she picked up the tray and started to walk out. At the door, she paused a second and said a few words to Moshe, again in Hebrew. Then, the door was closed.

Broward did not ask Moshe to translate his words with the woman. He knew that, if the cell was bugged, and it probably was, the monitor had asked for somebody in Pyotr's group, other than the woman, who knew Hebrew.

Moshe, guessing what Broward was thinking, put his hand on Broward's wrist, and he tapped out in code what he did not dare to say aloud.

"I was right. I knew her. She was the child of very good

friends of my parents when we lived in Ugolyak. I always suspected them of being Jewish, and I knew that if her parents had attempted to educate her as mine had tried to educate me, then she'd know Hebrew."

"So?" Broward tapped back.

"So . . . I was right. So, I'm not the only Hebrew left alive in the world."

"She doesn't have to be . . ."

"No, she doesn't. But I gave her the opening phrases of *Hatikvah*, the national anthem of Israel. It's long been a criminal offense to sing it, so if she knew it . . . well, she replied with the the second line."

Moshe sang softly, "'*Kolod balevav penimah*,' I said. And she answered, '*Nefesh yehudi, homiyah*.' Translated, 'Oh while within a Jewish breast beats true a Jewish heart.'"

"I still don't see . . ."

"But you'll see."

'But when they translate what you two said, she'll be in trouble. If you're planning on her help, you might as well forget about her."

"She's no dummy. Remember, she has a perfectly good excuse for talking to me in Hebrew. And I didn't ask her openly to help me. Just made some pleasantries, complimented her on her good looks. I didn't even remind her that we once knew each other. But she knows."

"Just what are you banking on?"

"That she'll think I'm a Jew and will help me."

"Are you or aren't you?"

Moshe shrugged and smiled. Then, he tapped, "I never wanted to be. But everybody insists that I am. Can the whole world be wrong?"

A half hour later the door swung open. This time, there were four armed soldiers. The woman, Katashkina, was not there. The two Moonmen were marched out and back to Pyotr's office. The huge dark man was still behind the desk. But the woman stood in front of it.

Pyotr said, "You presented a great problem. But Lieutenant Katashkina has suggested a plan with high probabilities of succeeding. Unfortunately, it involves your deaths and those of all on the Moon. I would rather not do this, but I have no alternative."

Pyotr looked at them intently as if expecting a violent reaction, but the two, frozen-faced, merely stared back. Pyotr smiled and then said. "There's no need my informing you what we're going to do, since your cooperation will be complete but involuntary. However, the lieutenant's plan is such a clever one that I can't resist telling it to you. It'll give you something to think about on the way back."

His plan was very simple, and, from his viewpoint, admirable in that it solved everything. It did not matter that it meant the deaths of three hundred people, perhaps the extermination of half the human race.

Broward and Yamanuchi were to be placed back inside their ship and in a state of stasis in their chairs. Only, this time, they would have no means to release themselves; they would be prisoners of the field until the ship crashed onto the Moon's surface at a velocity of 50,000 kilometers per hour.

The two would have company: the "planet-shaker" bomb, This would not be in the ship, since it was too large to fit inside, but would be attached to the vessel. It would have its own drive, and, at the proper moment, would release itself and dive at the moon. The inconceivably violent explosion would create a crater at least two hundred kilometers wide and fifty deep. The shock waves would not only shatter every base on the moon but would instantly kill every living being.

"To quote an old American proverb," said Pyotr, "we are killing two birds with one stone. We will not only remove the peril of attack by the Moon, we will take away any chance the Axe might have to find out about us from the Moon personnel."

Broward was stunned but he managed to protest.

"You monster! You are as evil as Howards!"

"Not at all," said Pyotr. "I am merely doing what I must do to make sure that I and my people survive. I am doing so reluctantly, but . . ."

"Can't you just join the Moon, become part of it, help us in our fight for survival against the forces of Nature and of Mars?"

"Your people are Communists," said Pyotr. "We have rejected that false doctrine, and we are determined to build a new society. We can do it because we have a small group that can be closely controlled. We can educate our children into Pyotrism with no chance of foreign and contradictory ideas being introduced to confuse them. Moreover, we have a chance to get rid of our enemies once and for all."

"But, there are some on the Moon who are not Communists!" said Broward. "I am one of them. For a long time

I've been a member of an underground known as the Athenians. Perhaps you've heard of them. Moreover, Moshe is not a Communist; he despises them. I—"

"You are not a Pyotrist."

He gestured at the two and said, "Take them away."

Broward and Moshe looked despairingly at him and then at the woman. She regarded them coldly and unflinchingly.

"I have never been so wrong about a woman in all my life," said Moshe as he and Broward were marched away.

They were not, however, taken at once to the ship. The Pyotrists had to compute and tape a new journey to the Moon, one for the ship and a different path for the bomb's motor after it separated from the ship. The process took three hours; meanwhile, the two sat in a small room near the undersea port. Broward tried to talk to the three guards, but they only told him to shut up. Oddly, he felt nothing at that moment but a longing for a cigarette. Now that he was to die soon, he did not see any reason to hold to his determination to quit smoking.

"At least give me a cigarette," he said.

"We don't have any," one of the guards said. "We've thrown them away. All liquor, too. We've gotten rid of all things that weaken the human body. Now, shut up!"

Broward sighed. He was indeed among fanatics.

"We could rush them, force them to kill us," said Broward in a low voice to Moshe. "We'd at least not die like chickens trussed up for the slaughter."

"If there was a chance of getting away from them," said Moshe, "I'd do it. But there isn't. No, we're not dead yet. Maybe we can do something when we're on the ship."

"Break out of stasis? You know better."

"I don't know better. All I know is that things have a way of coming up unexpected, unpredictable. It's like an unimaginably vast roulette wheel. You never know where the ball's going. True, the odds are in the House's favor, but you still have a chance to win."

"It's a shame that a man like you has to die," murmured Broward.

But he thought, Moshe is right. And as long as there are men like Moshe, man has a chance of surviving. There must be others like him, not only on the Moon and Mars and Ganymede and Mercury, but in this place under the sea on Earth and only God knew how many other places on Earth.

Only God knew. . . . how often that phrase was used in a supposedly Godless society by Godless men. Of course, its frequency was explained as being an archaic cliché, a figure-of-speech survival that did not mean anything.

Katashkina entered the room. She said, "Let's go. Everything's ready."

The two prisoners stood up and then marched out of the room with two men behind them and Katashkina and another guard several paces before them.

A car was waiting for them; this had a back seat over which a transparent bubble was placed. It was raised, and the two were forced to sit under it. The bubble was lowered and clamped magnetically. Katashkina and a guard got into the front seat, and the other two followed in another vehicle.

After that, events happened so swiftly that Yamanuchi and Broward were bewildered. The two cars shot down the tunnel and into the harbor. Here was a group of six men: a colonel, a captain, and four enlisted men. The car stopped. The bubble was raised. The prisoners were taken into their ship by Katashkina and two guards. The colonel and the captain started to follow them, but she said, "I am in charge. You two are not needed."

The colonel protested, but she said, harshly, "If you don't believe me, contact Pyotr. That is, if you want to take the chance of angering him. He doesn't like his orders questioned."

"I was told that I was in charge," the colonel said.

"Then the breakdown in communications should be investigated," she replied. "There's inefficiency and incompetency somewhere along the line."

The colonel scowled, but he stepped back. He was still looking perplexed when she shut the port.

The two guards were startled by this, but they said nothing. Nor did they speak when Katashkina pulled her automatic from her holster and ordered them to drop their weapons. Like the prisoners, they were stunned.

"No time to explain now," she said to Moshe. "Take the controls. Do as I say."

Moshe smiled as if he could not believe what was happening, but he obeyed. She then placed her finger on the button that actuated the port, and she said to the guards, "I'm opening this just far enough for you to squeeze out one at a time. Go!"

The first to the port, a large red-faced man, had to turn sideways to get through. For a second, he struggled, and

Katashkina opened the port a little more. Before he could take advantage of the increased space, there were shots from outside, and he fell back under the impact of the bullets. His legs, however, were sticking out of the ship.

"Take it away," she said. Moshe touched the controls, and the ship rose and sped across the harbor, then up. Katashkina glanced at her wristwatch. "The ports are set to allow us exit. If the settings aren't countermanded in time, we'll get away. If not . . . Broward, shove that body out. We have to close the port."

Broward leaped to do as she said. He raised the dead man with one motion and flung the corpse outwards. It fell forwards, and the port began to close.

"Dive!"

Moshe changed the course so abruptly that those standing fell to the deck. But she kept her gun on the guard, and he made no move to jump at her. Then, the craft struck the surface, and water flooded in and rose to their ankles before the port was entirely closed. It spurted through the narrowing space and drenched all within the cabin.

"We're through the tunnel and going up," said Moshe. The screen that showed the area above them portrayed the huge port sliding to one side; it shone dull and heavy in the lights of the beams.

"Pyotr will have gotten my note by now," Katashkina said. "I told him that if he doesn't let us out, I'll have no choice except to set off the bomb. We'll die, but so will everybody. He'll know I'm not bluffing. I also told him that we won't reveal what happened here to the Moon, that we have no intention of going there."

"What?" said Broward. "Where in hell do you think we can go?"

"I've been planning for some time on getting away," she said. "I don't like Pyotr, and I don't like his ideas for our brave new world. I pretended to agree with him in every particular. But he made me sick. Especially since I knew him more intimately than anybody. I should, I was his mistress. I'm carrying his child."

Moshe made a strangled sound, but he kept his eyes on the viewplates. By then, they were out of the tower and rising towards the surface. Broward said, "We've four seats. That means that, if we're to make any speed, we have to go into stasis. It's a good thing we got rid of the other guard. If we hadn't, where would we have put him?"

"I know," she said. "I was planning on getting rid of both, but I knew that the colonel and his men might lose their heads and fire at the first one to come out. So . . ."

"You're a cool one," said Broward. "What do we do about . . ." he looked at the man's name, on the label over the right breast . . . "Schwartz?"

"You have two choices and two only," she said to Schwartz. "'You can throw in your lot completely with us, forget forever about Pyotr. Or you can be put down on the surface. We can't take you back there. Nor, even if you succeeded in overpowering us and taking the ship back yourself, could you go back. Pyotr would think the ship would be an enemy, and he'd shoot first and investigate later."

Schwartz, a handsome youth with curly brown hair and big brown eyes, said, "I don't have any choice if I want to live. You know I'd die horribly if you put me down on the outside."

"You're still living," said Moshe. "All right, Katashkina, you must have something in mind."

"I had thought that you would be the one to say where we will go," she replied.

Moshe smiled as if he had known what she would say. "When I first saw you, I thought that God had shown me the way. He had chosen me, not because I was the best but because I was the only. Rather, he had chosen me as the half of a tool. The other was missing, and I did not know where it was. Then, I was sent here, and I found you. I rejoiced. I also was miserable. Despite myself, I was being forced to accept a role I didn't want. First, human beings insisted that I was a Jew. Them, I could fight against. But when God Himself, a God I told myself I hadn't believed in, when God insisted, then I surrendered. Here was a Jewess. One like me, perhaps, a woman who didn't want the role any more than I did but who was being turned into a path not of her own choosing by something greater than she."

"I know what you mean," she said, "even if the others don't."

"There is no voice out of the burning bush," continued Moshe. "There doesn't have to be. I've been shown things that have unmistakably pointed the way and told me what I was to do. I didn't want to; I rebelled; I scoffed at myself and at God. Yet, the . . . *still small voice* . . . call it what you will, told me."

"I know. Just as I knew that you would come and just as I knew what I would have to do when you came."

"I'm not even sure of all the ceremonies, the traditions," said Moshe. "I've forgotten much. And we don't have the Book."

"There's one on the ship," she said. "As a psychology officer, I had access to many things forbidden to the public. So, I placed the Book in the storage hold when I came aboard to make an official investigation. I wasn't questioned about the things I was doing here."

"And we have food enough for two for several months," he said.

"What can you do?" asked Broward.

"We're not going to Mercury or to Ganymede. Sooner or later, Scone is going to get into contact with them. If he found me there . . . it's true that there are caverns on Ganymede, but it would take a lot of equipment to furnish the means for living in them. And there's always the chance that the others there might find us.

"Now, there must be many places on Earth that have not been wrecked, underground places, I mean. And there is enough equipment on Earth, scattered here and there but still retrievable. And if the equipment is radioactive, we can decontaminate it. So . . ."

Ten hours later, they were in a place made to order, capitalized Made To Order, as Moshe said, and prepared for them . It was one of the thousands of undersea stations established by the U.S.S.W. for the little colonies of seafarmers engaged in harvesting the sea and raising food for the billions of mouths of the once overcrowded world. This was a few miles off the coast of Israel; it was still functioning, even if the occupants, for some reason, had left. The tanks in which many different species of fish and various aquatic mammals were kept were filled with living creatures. These would have been dead in a day or two, but the arrival of the human beings saved them.

"We can make it now," said Moshe. "And our sons and daughters can make it. Some day, we . . . they . . . can return to the surface, and can resume life on the soil of the Promised Land. Did you ever see such luck? Or is it just luck? You can laugh, Broward, but there is a Hand in this."

"I won't laugh," said Broward. "I don't feel like it. But what about me? I don't want to stay here. My life is up on the Moon. What about Schwartz? If you and Katashkina let me go back, and you know you can trust me, what about Schwartz?"

"Just worry about yourself. Katashkina and I will take care of him. We have to find a woman for him, and we can do that, for there must be more than one sea-farm with survivors. How do you like that? Man will some day come forth from the sea, just as he did millions of years ago, only this time he won't have to evolve. And off the coast of Palestine will come forth the submarine Hebrews. How do you like that?" And he laughed.

"Be serious for a while. I want to talk about me."

"I am serious. I am most serious when I laugh. All right, we'll talk about you. Wait until I find out what Schwartz is doing. I don't want to wonder what he's up to while we're in a conference."

Three hours later, Broward left the sea-farm in the scout craft. He rose through the smoke-filled atmosphere and, once above it, flew visually and with manual controls until he had put 1,000,000 kilometers between himself and Earth. Then, he set up the codes that would tell the automatic navigational equipment to determine the present parameters of the craft and the Moon and to tape the flight plan to bring him back to Clavius. He did not forget to punch in an emergency plan in case of unexpected but possible contingencies during the return.

However, nothing happened. He was challenged, and he replied with the correct code and landed at the proper berth. Once he had left the ship and entered the office of the sergeant on duty, he knew that the situation had changed very much since his departure.

"I got a line for you to Scone," said the sergeant.

"It's a private one."

Broward took the phone and said, "Broward here, sir."

"Did you get the bomb?" said Scone. He sounded as if every second counted.

"Yes, sir. Only Yamanuchi isn't with me."

There was a pause, then Scone said, "What happened?"

"We had an accident while we were getting the bomb out."

"Very well. You can give me the details later. When we have time. Just now the important thing is that you did get back with the bomb . . . even if you are late. Another half hour, you wouldn't have made it. The Axe would have had it, or they would have destroyed you and the bomb before they knew what a valuable prize you would have made."

"They're on the way here?"

"Yes. One of our autoscouts flashed the warning. A big fleet. Too big for us. So, we're evacuating."

"Where are we going, sir?"

"The sergeant will give you the proper instructions. Thanks for coming through with the bomb, Broward. But I knew that if anyone could do it, you could."

There was silence; he had been cut off. He wondered if Scone was not disappointed that the accident had happened to Yamanuchi instead of to him. More than probably. But the man of stone would accept the fact as a fact and would make his plans accordingly.

"We got fifteen minutes to get away," said the sergeant. "Plenty of time to get to the other side of the Moon."

"What's there?"

"A big bubble with space enough for every craft on the Moon, including the *Zemlya,* to hide in. There's only one trouble with being there. If the Axe stay here instead of going back to Mars, what do we do then? We'll be out of touch with the others, on our own."

Broward paused at the entrance to the tube leading to the ship.

"Where will the . . . others be?"

"Just after you left, the drillers, looking for water, broke into a tremendous cavern. It not only had a big body of frozen water, it had space enough for all three bases to hide in and then some. So, when Scone heard about the Axe, he ordered everybody to hide there. We've been busy working our tails off, getting all the equipment down there, moving the lab stuff, all the rest, anything that could be moved and wasn't too big to go through the tunnel.

"As soon as everything's ready, or even if it isn't, the bases are going to be blown up. The tunnel will be plugged up for a little distance so the Axe won't know one's been made. We're hoping they'll think the bases were destroyed by Axe agents or missiles. Or that they'll think we decided we couldn't hold them and blew them up before we took off for Mercury or Ganymede or parts unknown."

"What if the Axe fleet leaves a garrison behind?"

"Scone says we'll worry about that when it happens. Please, sir, let's get going. I got my orders."

"Wait!"

Broward turned at the cry of a familiar voice to see Ingrid Nashdoi running towards him. He took her into his arms and kissed her while her tears ran and she clung tightly to him.

Finally, when she had quit weeping, she said, "I disobeyed the orders. I waited here for you, hoping you'd come back in time. If you hadn't, I don't know what I would have done. Maybe just let myself be blown up with the base."

Broward looked at the nervous sergeant. "It's all right," he said. "She'll come with us."

"I don't know, sir."

"I do. We haven't time for anything else, anyway. Don't worry. I'll take the responsibility."

Within three minutes, they were in the ship and in stasis. The sergeant, at the controls, had lifted them up and was hurling them around the curve of the great body beneath. In ten minutes, they had entered under a great shelf of volcanic rock. A few seconds later, they were through a gigantic opening and within the cavern. The beams of the ship guided them to the side of the *Zemlya*, where the sergeant maneuvered until the entrance port locked onto one of the monster vessel's ports.

The port slid within the walls of the craft; there was a whoosh of air as pressure equalized between the two entrances.

"You go ahead and report, Sergeant," said Broward. "I have some checking to do here."

The sergeant said, "Yes, sir," and he left, but not without being able to keep a peculiar look from flitting over his features.

Looking after him, Broward wished now that he had not been given that half-hour hypnotic session by Katashkina. If all memory of the location of the underwater station had not been repressed, he could have seized this chance to take off with Ingrid and return to them. But he did not know where they were. He did remember what had happened during the trip down and back. He remembered being in the station. But, ten minutes after he had left the place in his craft, a post-hypnotic command had plunged deep into his unconscious anything to do with the whereabouts of the two. They were somewhere under the sea, but where?

As for the report of his venture to Scone, that, too, had been taken care of during the session. He had a very detailed and, he hoped, convincing story of the finding of the bomb, of the so-called 'accident,' of his return and the reasons for the delay thereof. Scone should have no reason to investigate. After all, Yamanuchi was now dead, and the goal of the trip, the bomb, had been secured.

"Ingrid," he said, "let's get married. Now!"

Her eyes widened, and she said, "But how can we do that?"

"You do want to, don't you?"

"You don't have to ask."

"Then, we'll get the commander of the *Zemlya* to give his permission. That's all that's necessary. We get his permission; we record the marriage on the ship's log; that's that."

"But Scone is the commanding officer. And . . ."

"But he can't be contacted. The situation is the same as if we were aspace."

"Radman's the captain of the *Zemlya*. He's too cautious; he wouldn't do this unless he got the word from Scone. He'd be too suspicious because we're in such a hurry. He'd want to wait."

"Maybe you're right. Very well. Stay here. I'll be back in a few minutes."

Ingrid waited impatiently. She walked around the narrow cabin, looked into the storage hold, checked the air flow, and lit up one of the six cigarettes she owned, the last six on the Moon as far as she knew. By the time she had finished it, she saw Broward walking in through the port. Behind him were two soldiers.

He said, "We need two witnesses; one of them must be a commissioned officer. Allow me to introduce you to my friends Lieutenant Fielding and Corporal Garbon. They're willing to sign the ship's log, my ship, as witnesses. As commander, I'm privileged to marry anyone aboard who so wishes."

Ingrid laughed and kissed him and then kissed Fielding and Garbon.

"Let's celebrate later," said Broward. "Right now, on with the ceremony."

He went to the instrument panel, pressed a button, and began to state, in the official language prescribed, his desire to marry, the date, the location, and all the details needed. Ingrid followed him. Afterwards, the two soldiers described their names, ranks, serial numbers, and the fact that they were witnesses to the marriage.

"We can do the thumbprinting later," said Broward.

Garbon brought a thin flask out from under his uniform and opened it. The others held out three thimble-sized cups, and he filled each with Scotch. Then he poured one for himself, and all looked to Broward.

He lifted his cup and said, "A toast to the new bride. May she have a long and happy life and bear many fine and happy children."

"Wait a minute," said Fielding. "You forgot to toast the Union."

"The Union of the Soviet World Republics?" said Broward. "I toast the Union. The Union of Man. May it have a long and happy life."

Afterwards, there were jokes, some of them very Rabelaisian and all about newly married couples. Ingrid blushed at some of them, and this pleased Broward, though he would have found it difficult to say why. Then, abruptly, Fielding handed him the flask and the two soldiers left. Quickly, Broward closed the port. He turned to Ingrid, took her in his arms, and said, "It's not the time or place I would have picked for a honeymoon. But you will have to admit it's unique."

"For just a little while," she murmured, "let's pretend that we're alone in the universe."

They were lucky, for no one disturbed them. No calls came over the receiver. Perhaps, everyone in the ships clustered together in the tremendous cavern were silent and motionless, sitting like rabbits in a hole and hoping that the wolves prowling outside would not notice the hole. Perhaps there were other lovers who had found a niche and were making love, thinking that this might be their last chance forever.

But there came the time when Ingrid and Broward could no longer pretend that there was no outside world. Reluctantly, they opened the port and entered the larger domain of the *Zemlya*. He went to the captain's cabin to make a belated report, and she went to the biological laboratory to determine if she were pregnant. Radman, a tall, thin man with unruly wheat-colored hair, either was not aware of what Broward had done or was purposely ignoring it. He gave him an official welcome and told him that all ship commanders were to meet within an hour for a conference. No, no news about the Axe had come in. At present, a small scouter, disguised as a boulder, was on top of a mountain which formed part of the crater around the Clavius base. But it would not return with a report until it was safe for it to move. And that would not occur until the Axe left—if they did.

Broward hastened to the biolab and met Ingrid just as

she was leaving. By her downcast expression, he knew what the results of the test had been.

"Don't worry," he said. "We'll try harder the next time— if that's possible."

"If there is a next time. I have a feeling that something bad is going to happen and very soon."

"We'll see how your so-called woman's intuition works out. I'll see you later. I have to attend a meeting. But don't expect much. I'm very tired. I've had about three hours' sleep in the last thirty, and those were very trying hours."

"Including our honeymoon?" she said, but she smiled.

"A man should be fresh and strong then, darling. I'll get some sleep—I hope—and then I'll see you."

He kissed her briefly on the lips and walked away. However, he was not to return as quickly as he had hoped. Radman had called his officers together to discuss their procedure in case the Axe fleet remained in full force. Broward did not see much sense in this. It would be better to find out first if the enemy had come to establish bases. Otherwise, why waste time. Perhaps, Radman was doing this to give them something to occupy their thoughts and keep them from getting jittery. In any case . . . the next thing he knew, he was being shaken awake by the captain seated next to him. Radman was glowering at him, but, before he could say anything, Broward apologized. Thereafter, he had to struggle to keep his eyes open during the seemingly unending discussion. He managed, although without contributing anything of his own.

After listening to anybody who cared to volunteer, and there were many dissenting opinions, especially from the Chinese, Radman made his decision. If the scout indicated that the Soviet must evacuate, then the fleet would make a run for it to Ganymede. On the way, a ship carrying the bomb Broward had brought back from Earth would approach close enough to Mars to launch it. The Axe fleet would find out about the destruction of their home base sooner or later. When it did, then it could either surrender to the Soviet or die when its supplies were exhausted. Or it could start digging in some place, the Moon or Mercury. In either case, the Axe would be vulnerable to attack.

Broward did not understand why it would not be much better strategy to send one ship with the bomb against Mars while the Soviet fleet remained holed up. Why expose it? Why not lie hidden until the Axe fleet found out that the

Martian colonies were destroyed? If Argentineans then decided to rebuild the Moon bases or to dig deep into the interior, they could be simultaneously attacked by the Soviets already within the Moon and the fleet now in this cavern.

Did Radman have some ambition of his own to become supreme leader of the survivors? Did he hope that the Axe would locate Scone's group and destroy it?

Broward did not know. But he felt too tired and disgusted to care much at the moment. Dismissed, he left the conference room and returned to the scout ship. There, he found Ingrid waiting for him. The sight of her renewed his desire. He did not get to sleep as soon as he had planned.

"Do you know," he said drowsily just before he sank away, "this is what people everywhere should be doing. They should be making love at night, and in the daytime they should be working for their loved ones. Not thinking about how to kill and to keep from being killed. Wouldn't it be nice if everybody was doing just that?"

"If they were, we wouldn't be here," she said. "None of this would have happened; the Earth would still be populated, have air pleasant to breathe, and . . ."

"But it's not a nice world. Rather, sometimes it is, but most of the time . . ."

He was awakened by a voice from the com. "Captain Broward! Captain Broward! Report at once to Commander Radman on the bridge! Lieutenant Nashdoi! Lieutenant Nashdoi! Report at once to Commander Radman on the bridge!"

He jumped up from the air-mattress, shook Ingrid until she roused, and began dressing. Once she understood what was happening, she put on her uniform, hastily combed her short hair, and followed him into the *Zemlya*. There was much activity aboard, with every one busy at work or trying to look as if he or she had something important to do.

"What's up?" Ingrid said to Broward as they entered the huge navigation room where the officers' conferences were held. Then, she stopped so suddenly that he bumped into her, and she gasped.

He did not need to ask her what had startled her. There, standing behind the commander's desk, taller and bigger than any man in the room, was Scone.

"How . . . how . . . ?" said Ingrid, but Broward gave her a

little nudge and said, "Don't be frightened. What can he do?"

Scone gave them one long look, his features impassive, then he said something to Radman. The commander spoke loudly, "Take your seats! Colonel Scone will address you!"

Broward guided Ingrid to a seat, for she still seemed stunned, and he sat down beside her. Not caring that it was an unmilitary action, he took her hand in his. But he continued examining Scone.

The big man's face was smudged with dirt; his uniform jacket was ripped down one sleeve. And his eyes were circled with the blue of fatigue.

His voice, however, was as loud and powerful as ever; he did not seem to have lost a whit of confidence or authority.

"You must be surprised because I am here. You thought I was with the others in the refuge. And so I was. And how I got here is not important, because I made sure before we sealed up the main entrances to our cavern that there would be at least one exit. Its location is a military secret and will remain so until circumstances dictate otherwise."

By then, the entire audience was in a state of frenzied speculation, though silent, and many were semi-stunned. It seemed obvious that something terrible had happened and that Scone was the only survivor.

He gave one of his rare smiles and said, "I know what you are thinking. But you are only half right. The others are not lost—at least, not all of them, by any means. What happened is this . . ."

The Moonmen had entered the titanic bubble and had set off the chemical reactions that would melt down the bases and glass over the rocky floors. They did not dare destroy the bases with the small atomic bombs available because the Axe fleet was so close—it might have detected the explosions and certainly would have noticed the too-high radioactive background. Then, beams had melted the rock that formed the entrance tunnel. This was done to prevent the Axe detecting the tunnel with magnetometer readings. Because Clavius was in the sun's shadow, the hot rock on the surface would cool quickly, quickly enough so that the Axe would not notice the heat—it was hoped.

Then, the Moonmen waited. They were not inactive, however, for all hands were busy moving equipment to suitable places and to set it up. Since this bubble was to be the permanent habitation of most of them, the oxygen-generators had to be operated full blast. The water had to be melted. Construction of buildings was started. Rock was chewed up and blown into the machines that would convert the minerals therein into edible, though tasteless, food. Other rocks were broken down into fine particles and mixed with chopped-up garbage to make soil into which plants could fix their roots. Sunlamps were set up to beam on the plants, and water was sprayed over the ground.

During this, Scone kept watch. Above him, on the surface, was a boulder. Set within the boulder was a TV tube, the exterior surface of which looked just like lunar rock. A wire ran from the boulder beneath the rock and down into Scone's hiding place. He watched the Axe fleet approach warily. Their automatic scouts had already tested the defenses of the bases and found them wanting. They had also relayed the information that all the bases on the Moon seemed to be in ruins. Nevertheless, the first wave was composed only of gunboats which carried a few men and much detection apparatus of various kinds. The scouts poked around the shattered and melted fragments for an hour. But they must have signaled that all was well, for the big ships began to arrive.

Even so, if the vessels at Clavius were any indication of the number that landed at the other bases, then half of the Martian fleet must still be somewhere far above the Moon. Scone had no time to continue his surveillance, for he was called away. (By this statement, Broward guessed that Scone's post was not within the big bubble. That is, if he were telling the truth. The rest of his story made Broward wonder if the first part had conformed to reality.)

The officer communicating with Scone had reported that the Chinese element had attacked the others. They were using lasers, machineguns, grenade lobbers, and handguns. The onslaught had been entirely unexpected—by the Russians, that is, for Scone had not trusted any non-Americans even at this critical time. So, the Americans on guard warned the others immediately, and the Russian contingents had received the full force of the attack. Fully half of them were casualties in the first two minutes. But, vicious as the Chinese had been, they must have been making an effort to save the women for themselves. A third of these escaped to the American lines—if it could be said that there was any such thing as a 'line' in that melee.

Scone, on hearing the news, did not hesitate. He pressed

the button that sent pulses to the activation mechanisms of the three neutron bombs buried under the surface of each crater floor, of Clavius, Eratosthenes, and Fracastorius. For the second time within three weeks, a large proportion of the human race died. The soldiers and sailors of the Axe dropped where they stood. The beauty of this arrangement, as Scone made clear, was that the ships and equipment were left unharmed, available for use by the Moonmen.

Then, Scone hastened with a party of soldiers (so, thought Broward, he was not alone nor was he unprepared) to the bubble. All wore gravpaks and they got to their position quickly. This was an outcropping near the top of the cavern; on it was placed a powerful laser. Using this and the advantage of being able to see everything and everybody by the light of flares, they first put the Chinese big lasers out of commission. Afterwards, they destroyed the machine guns and grenade-lobbers and their crews. Most of the Chinese, though they realized they were defeated, fought to the end.

When it was over, all the Oriental men were dead or too badly wounded to keep battling. Ten Chinese women, however, were captured. Their enemies also wanted sexual mates and breeding stock.

At this moment, Broward realized consciously what he had only felt before as an undefined lack. That is, no Chinese personnel had been summoned to the meeting. This meant that Scone's next move would be to arrest and imprison them. Perhaps, they were even now in custody, though it did not seem likely because he would need his officers to carry out the move.

By then, despite the fact that the assembly was a formal military one, the room was in an uproar. Many of the Russians present were weeping or crying out questions to Scone. Some, however, sat in their chairs and kept their faces impassive. Broward wondered if these were not having the same doubts as he, that Scone had been the aggressor and had struck a blow to get rid of his opposition. Whatever their thoughts, they were keeping them to themselves. They wanted to continue to live; perhaps, to get revenge if their suspicions were proven valid later on.

Broward felt sorry for them because they were human beings. But, as an American whose country had been weakened by treachery and insidious cold-warfare, then violently conquered and savagely treated after defeat, he felt that they were getting what they deserved. If Scone had been treacherous and deadly, he had learned from masters in such.

Not that Broward approved of what he did. At this time, when so few men and women were alive and every one was needed, a blow against anyone was a blow to the whole species. Yet, he understood why Scone had acted so—if he were guilty.

Scone shouted above the tumult until he succeeded in quieting them.

"It has happened, and, regret it as we may, we cannot undo it. Nor can we rest. The enemy within has been conquered. The enemy without still lives, although he, too, has suffered greatly. However, he can afford to suffer more than we can, since his numbers are greater. And, now he knows that we are not out of the battle, he will begin searching the Moon, although he will do so very cautiously. He cannot turn tail and run back to Mars. Of course, he must consider the possibility that our bases were almost wiped out but that the few survivors left booby traps for the Axe. He'll consider this, but it won't make any difference to him. If he thought there was only one Soviet left alive on the Moon, he'd not rest until that lone survivor was dead or in chains.

"If the Axe search very thoroughly, they're bound to detect this cave. But it will take much time. Time is what we need, and what we'll get. Time to send the planet-shaker bomb to Mars and annihilate all our enemies except those who are spaceborne. As soon as that is done, we inform the Axe fleet and give them a choice of surrendering or fighting. If they decide to battle, they will have to deal not only with us but with the Ganymedans and Mercutians. Some hours after I received the report of the approaching Axe fleet, I sent emissaries to each of those bases to ask for help. I am sure that, once they realize the stakes, they'll send every ship they can."

Unless, thought Broward, they realize that what has happened to Scone's enemies here may eventually also happen to them. But, no, they would not know because the battle within the Moon had taken place after they left. Still, if they were as suspicious of Scone as he was of everybody else, they might refuse. Or, there might not even be anybody alive on the moon of Jupiter or the planet nearest the sun. The Axe might have taken care of them before they converged on the Moon.

A Russian, four seats from Broward, suddenly leaped up

and screamed, "You treacherous dog! You planned this! You want to kill all those who are not Yankees! Die! Die! Die!"

He pulled an automatic from his holster and fired at Scone. The big man dropped behind his table. Broward shoved Ingrid down on the floor and jumped at the Russian. The man had gone mad, his mind snapped, for he fired once again at the prone figure of Scone and then began to shoot at those nearest him.

The other Russians, perhaps fearing that the pistol shots meant that they were to die like the Chinese, pulled their weapons out. Those nearby, not too stunned to move, responded. The chamber was filled with the booming of guns, the shrieks of wounded men, the hoarse cries of men shouting in hysteria and fear. There were scuffles as men seized the Russians and tried to drag them down; some of these fell, struck by bullets from their own comrades, who were firing in a frenzy.

Abruptly, it was all over. Most of the Russians lay silent. But the melee had cost the others even more heavily. Fifteen Russian dead; twenty Americans and Europeans dead or badly wounded.

Broward, untouched by bullets, made his way through the shouting people until he found Ingrid. She was sitting on the floor, white-faced, and was staring at him with enormously wide eyes.

"You all right?" he said.

She shook her head to indicate that she was not harmed. He had to sit down then, for he found himself shaking violently. It was some time before he could control himself. "God," he moaned to Ingrid, "if this keeps up, we'll destroy ourselves."

Ingrid started to answer but closed her mouth. She pointed, and Broward, looking in the indicated direction, saw Scone standing up on the platform behind his desk. His face was pale, but he did not seem to be wounded. The energy and authority he showed within the next few moments were not those of an injured man.

"Now, have you seen enough!" he shouted. "Do you need any more convincing? Our enemies have conspired from the beginning to kill us off so that they could inherit the world. They have failed. But our job is not yet complete.

"You, Radman, detail men to arrest all Chinese, men and women. Put all Russians under arrest, too. Place them in the SA tanks!"

He was referring to the suspended amimation chambers in which it had originally been planned to put the personnel of the *Zemlya* during the many years that it would take to reach Tau Ceti. This action, thought Broward, was at least humane. He had expected Scone to order all the male Russians and Chinese executed.

"Don't worry," said Scone to the unvoiced questions of many. "Later, when we have defeated the Axe, we will remove the women from the tanks. And the men also will be released, but much later and one at a time so that we may evaluate their trustworthiness, their ability to integrate with us after they have been properly deconditioned."

He looked at Broward. "You! Go to my office and wait there for me."

Broward said softly to Ingrid, "Let me handle this. I'm sure he doesn't know we're married. I'll break the news."

He walked away and entered the office. Not wishing to give Scone the feeblest excuse for trouble, he did not sit down but stood before Scone's desk, ready to spring to attention when he came in. It was a long wait, only ten minutes by his wristwatch but interminable by other standards. Finally, when Broward was beginning to wonder all sorts of things, even that Scone was angry enough to accuse him of treachery, the commander walked in. He strode to his desk, sat down, placed his big hands on the desk, and looked at Broward grimly.

"So," he said, "we have taken one more step towards the defeat of our enemies. Now, give me a report of your trip to Earth. Make it brief, however. I know that you came back with the bomb."

Broward told his story, the false and true details spilling out easily. Scone kept his pale blue eyes fixed on Broward's face as if he were trying to read behind the flesh. Then, when Broward ended with the account of his ship's landing at the port of Clavius, Scone seemed to relax a trifle. He leaned back and said, "It couldn't have gone better."

By which Broward knew that Scone was pleased not only with the retrieval of the bomb but the solution of the problem of the "Jew." At that moment, Broward hated Scone as never before. He even thought of killing him, but he did not act on the thought. If he did so, he would be as much a monster as Scone. Moreover, he himself would undoubtedly be executed a few minutes later. No, he wanted to live, to enjoy life with Ingrid, and to ensure the survival of mankind—although he was doubtful that mankind was really worth saving.

He did derive a bitter satisfaction from the knowledge that Moshe was safe and that Scone, although he would never know it, was cheated.

"We have the bomb," said Scone. "How do we use it?" He was speaking out loud to himself, for he would never have asked Broward for advice. "This mission to deliver the bomb must not fail. It is our greatest, I might almost say, our only chance to defeat the Axe."

He glared at Broward. "You realize that I cannot go on this expedition. I cannot trust these people. Some of them might try to take over while I'm gone."

"I know," murmured Broward.

"I need somebody who has proven himself."

"Me?"

"You will have to admit that, logically, you are the candidate."

Broward nodded his head and thought, If I complete the mission but should die while doing it, then Scone, once again, will have killed two birds with one stone. And I will be the means of the murder that I hate, the instrument of the murder that I hate.

"Like it or not," continued Scone, "I have to spare one ship. That will be the one that already has the bomb attached to it. Hmm. I made a mistake. I should have ordered you, once you had the bomb, to proceed to Mars with it. Then, it would all be over. No, it wasn't a mistake. I had to know for sure that you did get it."

"I am not a professional navigator," said Broward.

"That does not matter. You know enough to get there. In this day of automatic devices, a man does not have to be highly skilled to pilot a spaceship. If he knows enough to feed the proper data into the computer . . . we will program most of the flight. I can't spare more than one man."

"So much depends on the success of this," said Broward. "You can't afford to take a chance. We can't afford . . ."

"One man, one ship," replied Scone firmly. "Two men won't help. It wouldn't help if I sent my entire fleet out with you. In fact, the fewer in space, the less chance of detection."

"Sir," Broward said, "I request permission to take along my wife!"

"Your . . . wife? I didn't know you were married?"

"Ingrid Nashdoi and I were married shortly before you showed up, sir."

"Who gave you permission? I specifically . . ."

Scone's voice trailed off, but Broward knew what he meant to say.

"*I* did," said Broward. "It's legal."

"Why should you want to take her along? It's a very dangerous mission."

"If either of us were to die, the other wouldn't want to live. If we have to die, then let it be together."

Broward hoped that Ingrid would agree with him; he was sure that she would.

Scone's lips curled and he said, "All very sentimental, I'm sure: I might say, the sentiments of a bourgeois."

"That is the way we feel, sir."

"Broward, you know that the life of every woman is precious. The future of the race depends upon her. If I sanctioned this stupid senseless move, I would be betraying my trust, the survival of mankind."

"Very noble sentiments, sir. Those of a true leader, who is devoted to his species."

"None of your sarcasm. What I have done, I have done to ensure peace in the future and a life worth living. No, Broward, your request is not granted. No! Would you like to sit down? You look faint."

"I'll stand. How do we proceed, sir?"

"You must be tired. Go rest. I want you to be in as fine a shape as possible, since you have an extremely grueling task ahead. We will set up the flight and make the ship ready. You will be awakened."

Broward saluted and turned to leave, but Scone said, "Oh, yes. You must not be disturbed. I'll station a guard so you won't be bothered by visitors."

"I understand," said Broward. Furious, but helpless, he walked away. When he had gone through the conference room, instead of obeying his orders, he went to the biolab to look for Ingrid. She should be taking care of the "freezing" of the Russian and Chinese prisoners. He found her at the controls of a large console, making some adjustments needed for the preliminary "treatment" of those about to be frozen. These were out of sight in another room, but he was familiar enough with SA procedure to know that they had been put to sleep with an anaesthetic gas.

He bent over her as if he were asking her a question about

her work and said softly, "Keep on working, Ingrid. And don't look surprised or alarmed. I've been ordered to deliver the bomb to Mars. I'm not supposed to see you; I'm supposed to be resting."

Ingrid continued to watch the indicator lights and meters on the panel. She said, "Mars! Why didn't you ask Scone if I could go with you? You know . . ."

"I knew, and I did ask. He refused."

"Can't you say no? Tell him you will not go?"

"You know better than that. He'd either have me shot or else placed in the tanks with the others."

"Couldn't I stow away?"

"Not a chance. Scone will make sure of that."

"Isn't there anything we can do?"

"We can hope. First, the Axe must be destroyed. Afterwards, who knows what will happen? I've seen things take too unexepcted a turn to think that Scone will always have his way."

"I want to go with you to your room at least."

"That you will, if I have anything to do with it. Get somebody to take your place. I'll wait for you outside."

He left and stood outside the entrance for a minute. Ingrid came then, saying, "I told Miller that my orders were to be with you during the little time left before you took off."

"Now to find the guard before he reports to Scone. I'll brazen it out with him. He can't be so hard-hearted he'd refuse to let you stay with me."

So it was. The guard was so relieved that he had not lost Broward that he was very receptive. His orders had been to conduct Broward to a certain room and then stand at the door, to let no one in after Broward had entered. However, the order had said nothing about anyone who might enter at the same time he did or who went in before him. Thus, Broward paused a second to give Ingrid precedence and followed. The guard closed the port, and they were alone.

Four hours later, the port opened. The guard said, "The Colonel wants to see you in the briefing room."

Broward kissed Ingrid. "It's good-bye now. Or, as the Axe says, *hasta la vista*. Give me another kiss."

"*Hasta la vista*, sweetheart. I'll do what you said while you're gone."

He looked back once at the branching of the corridor and waved. She smiled and waved back, but he was sure that, as soon as he was out of sight, she would run weeping back into the room. He felt tears forming over his own eyes.

In the briefing room, Scone and the officers concerned with the business of getting him to Mars were examining the map projected on the wall by a wristwatch-sized box. Scone turned from it and said, "You don't look very rested."

Broward saluted and said, "I didn't feel like sleeping."

"Your briefing will not be so brief. About one and a half hours."

He seemed jubilant; he was even smiling. Could he be so happy at the possibility of getting rid of his competition with Ingrid? No, it would take something more than the chance of winning a woman to unthaw that glacier of a man.

"While you were supposed to be resting," said Scone, "I have been working. And you'll be pleased to know that, when you take off, there'll be something to divert the Axe, to take their minds off chasing you."

Broward looked puzzled. Scone grinned exultantly and said, "When the neutron bomb was detonated at Clavius, the ports of the vessels that had landed there were still open after releasing the inspection teams. I took note of that and also of the fact that the landings of the other parts of the fleet at Eratosthenes and Fracastorius were synchronized with those at Clavius. So, the ports of the other ships should also be opened. After we subdued the Chinese, I made arrangements with my men before I left for this place.

"I have just received a report from them. They have gained entrance to the ships at Clavius. They have familiarized themselves with the controls of the vessels and are ready to move against the ships now in orbit above the Moon. The small ships will carry some men to Eratosthenes and Fracastorius; these will try to enter the craft there."

A captain said, "How do you like that? Using their own ships against them? And it'll be a complete surprise to them!"

"So, we're not going to hide like rats in a hole, waiting for word from you before we dare scuttle out," said Scone. "We're going out to battle the Axe. And you will have a much better chance of getting away undetected during the fight. Even if a ship spots you, it's going to be too busy with our battlebirds to get involved with an insignificant scout."

He sobered and said, "Unfortunately, an enemy detected the scout that reported to me. It called in three other ships, and they are now cruising around this area. Undoubtedly, they're using magnetometers and will find this bubble.

But, at the rate they're going, they won't be near here for another two and a half hours. Plenty of time to get you prepared and for the birds to get ready for battle. Every ship we have, except the *Zemlya*, of course, is in this."

"And so we go forth," said Broward. "We may return behind our shields, but, if we lose, there will be no one to carry us back on our shields."

"What?" said Scone. "What did you say? Sometimes Broward . . ."

"Never mind. What is the plan?"

Two hours later, Broward sat at the controls of his ship. It lay in line behind three battlebirds. Behind him the other vessels of the fleet were arranged in order.

Outside was darkness and the blazing many-colored eyes of the sky, most of them blotted out by the towering bulk of the cruiser in front of him. The floor of the bubble sloped away downwards from its mouth so that the noses of the spaceships on the floor pointed upwards. But the entrance was set halfway up the side of an immense mountain, and, on the ledge outside, a TV camera, hidden inside a pseudo-boulder, transmitted a picture of the three enemy vessels. These were separated by a distance of two kilometers each and were proceeding parallel to each other at a very slow pace towards the bubble.

"One minute to go," said Scone's voice from a transmitter set in the arm of Broward's chair. "When the buzzer is activated, the *Washington, Jefferson,* and *Roosevelt* will proceed as directed.

"Broward, five seconds after the *Roosevelt* has launched, you will launch at an initial velocity of 1000 kilometers per hour and will hold down the full-acceleration button until you think you are safe. The second sounding of the buzzer will be your signal to go into action."

He thought, "Ingrid, will I ever see you again?" and then the first buzz sounded. Suddenly, the three great bulks were gone.

He counted so slowly that the buzzer came again before he had voiced the "four." At the command of his fingers, which were operating the controls on a small swinging panel at chest-height, the scout rose. He pushed the velocity stick forward to the designated mark. No sensation of the cavern's rock walls sliding by or of the mouth flying at him. Suddenly, he was out above the moon, or, at least, he supposed he was, for he could not see it. Without thinking about the move, still slightly bewildered by the change, he depressed the FA button. And, as quickly as he had left the bubble, he was out of the shadow and in the sunlight. In the plates showing him the view from 'behind' and 'below,' the Moon was dwindling fast, shooting away from him. And there was nothing on the radar to indicate that any objects were in pursuit of him.

He began to activate the various controls needed to initiate the program for sending him Marsward. The equipment in the ship was already determining its approximate location by radar and by light: the relative positions and angles of the Moon, Earth, Sun, and several stars. Though he was not aware of it, except by observation of the panel indicators, the ship had changed course and was on the path that would take it to its destination. Broward remained in the chair. He could not leave it until he turned off the stasis field and he could not do that, without committing suicide, until he had slowed the scout down to an acceleration he could endure. There was no need for that now; the best policy was to allow the ship to travel at top speed until he had to shut off stasis. If he must perform natural functions such as eating, and excreting, he had the facilities for those in various compartments in the chair. Sleeping was also done there. He wished that he could have been in a larger vessel, for these provided for complete facilities. Some of the higher officers in the big ships even had small cabins enclosed in stasis during the dangerous speeds. The only drawback was that the larger the stasis, the more power was required, and all objects within the field were in free fall. Scoutships, to conserve fuel, restricted stasis to as small an area as possible.

He sat in the chair, ate a little when he felt hungry, slept, did some exercising, making sure that during it his body did not come into contact with the field. In the viewplate, polarized to dim the full glory, the sun grew larger. It raved and ravened; tongues of flame shot upwards, blazing globes large as the continent of America were hurled outwards, then fell back, aborted worlds. Fascinated and fearful despite his knowledge that the ship's speed war greater than the escape velocity required, Broward watched the sun for hours. It was so inconceivably huge and violent that he felt an awe approaching that which the primitive sun-worshippers must have experienced. Perhaps, his exceeded theirs, for he was closer to the terribleness of it.

Then, it began to shrink and to drift towards the right of

the viewplate. Then, it was gone. And he knew that he had 78 hours to go.

Five times during that period he decelerated to the point at which he could shut off stasis. At 1.2 G, he walked around the narrow confines of the cabin and even crawled around into the storage hold to give himself much-needed exercise. He did pushups and kneebends until he was panting and was so tired that he had no trouble falling asleep. He talked to himself and he listened to music and drama and poetry from the pocket player. At times, he felt he would go mad if he did not have a cigarette, but he did not.

Endlessness. Loneliness. Insignificance.

But these came to an end as the globe of Mars merged from a bright star into a tiny planet. Before then, he had again begun to decelerate. Not because he was supposed to, for that was not the plan. It was intended that he should approach in a great curve and come in at a tangent towards the nightside of Mars. Although the Axe would undoubtedly have detection stations on that side, they would not expect attackers to be coming from that direction. Actually, they should not expect any, for they must believe by now that, if there were any Soviet survivors, approach to Mars would be the last thing in their minds. Unless, of course, the Axe had destroyed the Ganymedan base and might think that this object contained Soviets who had been away on an expedition. Returning and finding the base gone, they might have come to Mars to surrender. Or, conceivably though not probably, the Soviet ship was making a kamikaze run with the hopes of destroying at least one Martian colony.

Whatever the Axe reaction, Broward was curving out towards the nightside.

But he found himself reluctant to replace the scout in the programmed path. This, despite the fact that the longer he waited, the more chance he gave the Martians to locate him and send ships and missiles or both against him. He knew that he must launch the bomb and that the sooner he did it, the better for him and the success of his mission. Yet, he could not bring himself to start.

A buzzer sounded; a red light began flashing on the instrument panel. Startled, he looked at the various radar-scopes and saw that one had a blip. A piece of cosmic debris? An Axe ship? He pressed a button on the panel, and a piece of paper slid out of a narrow slot. On it was printed the distance, direction relative to the ship, speed, and approximate size of the target. It was about four hundred and eighty kilometers away, was proceeding on a path parallel to his, was on the same heading, traveling at 45,000 kilometers per hour, and was about three times the size of his scout.

His first impulse was to throw his craft into full speed and then towards a ninety-degree angle from the stranger. But his hands remained poised before his chest. Why was he waiting? He did not know. There was something emanating— if he could use the word in such an unscientific term—from the object. What? There was no defining it except as a call for help. Despite any evidence whatsoever, he felt that someone was crying out for aid. Although he had never considered himself to be in the least receptive to psychic phenomenon—if such indeed existed—he was now experiencing something akin to it. Whatever it was, it was reaching him through no ordinary channels of communication.

His third impulse was to continue with the first. The long isolation and strain had unnerved him, might even be causing hallucinations. If he succumbed, he would not only die, but, eventually, Ingrid and all his comrades would. No. He would pay no attention to the voiceless shout.

He reached down. Instead of pushing on the velocity stick, he pressed two controls. These activated the frequency-finders for the radio and laser receivers. Several seconds passed while he watched the scopes for evidence that the object had changed course, was increasing speed, or had released a second unknown object against him. None of these occurred, and then the radio receiver, having located and locked onto a certain continuing frequency, burst into life.

A voice was speaking in Spanish, a man's voice.

It had been some time since Broward had spoken Spanish. At first, he did not understand. But the man was obviously repeating the same phrases over and over. Within a minute, Broward understood him. He *was* calling for help. He was Lieutenant Pablo Quiroga, and he was in the communications section of what was left of the cruiser *Juan Manuel de Rosas*. The *de Rosas*, with two destroyers, had detected and then pursued the remnants of the fleeing South African fleet. (Though Quiroga did not say so, his words implied that Howards, the Argentinean dictator, had done to his allies what Scone had done to the Russians and Chinese. Except that in this case there was no doubt about Howards' treachery.)

The South Africans had turned around to fight or, perhaps, the Argentineans had intercepted them. Whatever had happened, the result of the battle had been the annihilation of the South African ships. But at a heavy cost. Both destroyers had been shattered by missiles. The *de Rosas* had finished off the African dreadnought but had been sliced through in several places by lasers. Quiroga had survived in the sealed-off section. He did not know if there were others also living in similar sections. But he was calling Mars or any ships that might be in the neighborhood. He could not last long. He was out of food and water, and the air would give out in another three hours or less.

Broward, having adjusted the transmitter to the frequency received, said in Spanish, "Lieutenant Quiroga. Lieutenant Quiroga. How long have you been broadcasting?"

There was a pause. Then, Quiroga answered in such a torrent that Broward could understand only a phrase and a word here and there. He waited until the man had finished speaking and said, "Speak more slowly."

"You are not an Argentinean," replied Quiroga. "I can tell by your pronunciation. What are you? A South African survivor? God help us, are you in the same situation as I am?"

"Not quite," said Broward. He hesitated to identify himself, because it was possible that Axe ships were even now on the way in response to Quiroga's call. He said, "Are your lasers working? If so, turn one on. I'll lock into it."

"Go ahead."

"Now," said Broward, "we can talk without anyone eavesdropping. I am Captain Broward of the lunar base of Clavius."

There was another silence, so long that Broward decided the other fellow was afraid to reply. He said. "I don't intend to harm you. In fact, I will take you aboard. But only as my prisoner."

"A Soviet prisoner?" said Quiroga. He began to laugh uncontrollably. Broward sat quietly until the man had started to sob. Then, he said, "I'm sure that we can find a place for you in our society, a quite agreeable place. If you're co-operative, that is."

He did not say anything about the necessary period of suspended animation into which Quiroga would be placed nor that it might be years before he would be 'unfrozen.'

"I don't understand," said Quiroga. "What are you doing out here? And where would you take me? I thought . . . I thought that . . ."

"That your fleet had annihilated those on the Moon and Ganymede?"

"Ganymede is untouched. El Macho intends to take the Ganymedans prisoners later; they don't have defenses worth considering. They're ripe . . ."

"For the plucking. Well, thanks for the information. As for the Moon, the less you know, the better for everybody. Do you want to come aboard?"

"If I stay here, I will surely die. If I become your prisoner . . . ? Why do you want me?"

Broward could not answer that to his own satisfaction. He intended to loose a weapon that would instantly slay anywhere from 500 to several thousand men, women, and children. Yet, he was risking all to save a single enemy from death.

"I can't come in after you," he said. "You'll have to enter willingly and unarmed into my ship. If you don't reply immediately, I will be forced to leave at once."

"I surrender. And I give you my word of honor as an Argentinean and a Christian that I will not bear arms or try force."

Broward smiled grimly on hearing that and began the steps that would result in automatic placing of his vessel near that of the wreck. After that, he would take over manually. The process required time, more time than he really thought he could afford. But he could not abandon Quiroga. Somehow, by rescuing him, he was compensating for what he would do to his fellows. The idea was not logical or even rational. One life for thousands was ridiculous. But he felt that he was making some slight payment and that was better than none at all.

Fortunately, or unfortunately, depending upon which way he cared to look at it, there was a port in the section in which Quiroga was trapped. It was not difficult to match the course and speed of his ship with the section. The wreck looked like a huge drum, for the lasers of the South Africans had neatly carved on both sides, as if a section of a sausage had been cut out. The drumshape was not revolving, and this was the reason that Quiroga had been able to make the tight laser-beam contact with Broward. The lack of spin made it relatively easy to jockey the scout next to the gigantic port, which was designed to admit even larger ships than his.

For a moment, watching the big door shut, Broward was uneasy. But he knew that his own beams could melt a hole through the walls for an avenue of escape, and it did not seem likely that Quiroga would want to try anything. Not at this time, anyway.

The inner port opened, and a man in a spacesuit walked through. By this, Broward knew that the means for flooding the landing-port with air were not available. He opened his own port, gave the Argentinean enough time, and closed it. After filling the little chamber with air, he said over the speaker, "Take off your suit. Then come in with your hands over your head."

Without waiting for the man to finish unsuiting, Broward took the scout out of the port and away towards Mars. He accelerated slowly to one G so that Quiroga would not have difficulty maneuvering. Then, after placing the controls in automatic, he picked up a pistol, and opened the inner port. Lieutenant Pablo Quiroga entered. He was dressed in silver coveralls with scarlet crossed axes on the right chest and silver bars on the shoulders. He was tall, well-built, about thirty, had a ruddy skin, handsome face, greenish-brown eyes, and wavy deep-brown hair.

He spoke a passable American English. "Where do you intend to take me?"

"Right now you're just going along on the ride," his captor replied. "Sit down in the chair to my left. Here's some stiktite. Wrap it around your ankles so they'll be bound together. Then place your hands behind you, and I'll tape your wrists."

The prisoner did as he was told and presently was bound and seated to Broward's satisfaction. The American then got a flask of water, which Quiroga drank eagerly. After he had enough, he ate the food which Broward spooned from a can and gave to him.

"Nobody's fed me like that since I was a child," remarked Quiroga. "Just now, I feel as helpless as a baby."

"But you're not a baby. I'll remember that. O.K. I'm going to sit down in a moment. When I do, I'll place a stasis field around both our chairs. You know what 'stasis' means in English?"

Quiroga nodded.

"O.K. Watch yourself."

Quiroga watched the forward visual plate for a while. As if he could not believe it was happening, he said, "You are heading for Mars?"

"I don't plan to land there."

"Then what . . . ? You plan to missile one of the bases? That will be suicide! Or do you plan on that, too?"

"Do you think I would have bothered to rescue you then?"

"Not unless you are a sadist," Quiroga said. "But you don't act like one."

Broward debated whether or not he should tell the Argentinean what type of bomb he was carrying. After a little thought, he decided against it. The fellow might go mad and do something wild, something to disturb the smooth progress of the ship. If he touched the field, he would be sucked through and spread like a red film all over the interior of the cabin.

"You might as well have left me back there," Quiroga said after a silence. "But I am happy that you did not. At least, I had a drink of water and food. And somebody to talk to, even if he is a Soviet. Death, when it comes, will not find me alone."

Broward glanced at him and said, "I think that if we had met under different circumstances, in a different world, we might have liked each other."

"Who knows? It is very possible. I do not hate Americans. My mother was half-American. But the Soviets . . . !"

"I am a Soviet citizen. Outwardly, at least. Listen! I want to tell you some things, some true things."

Many times, Quiroga opened his mouth to protest, but each time Broward told him harshly to shut up, to wait until he, Broward, was finished. If he did not obey, then he would have his mouth taped.

After half an hour, Broward was through with his narration. Then, he quit talking, fully expecting a rage of denial. But Quiroga, strangely, was silent for some time. When he did speak, his voice had a thoughtful tone and sounded very unsure.

"Howards told us that it was the South Africans who set off the cobalt bombs. At first, he said that they could not really be blamed, that the Axis was too small and too weak to fight the whole world. That the only reason we had not been overrun before was the threat to use the C-bomb if war was waged against us.

"But, once the South Africans had exploded them, we could do nothing but make the best of a very bad situation. There was still hope for us. Though Earth was dead, it would not always be so. Meanwhile, we could rid the solar system of the evil ones who had started this, exterminate those responsible for this monstrous evil, this sin against man and God. And we could establish a new society on Mars unhindered by enemies without or within."

Broward winced at the latter sentence. It sounded so much like his own words.

"But there was some very carefully guarded talk, hints, that Howards himself had given the order to use the bombs. Also, there were things here and there that one picked up. These didn't mean much when each item was isolated. However, if you put them together, an ugly picture began to form.

"I knew this, but I rejected the idea. Then, we officers and later the noncoms were called into conferences. We were told there was evidence that the Africans were plotting treachery. If they were to get rid of us, then they'd have the solar system all to themselves. It would become a black world or, at least, a brown one. The Africans would, of course, spare the women and have children by them. These lectures, of course, were to prepare us for the attack against our allies. Howards reasoned that we must jump first. And we did.

"He also revealed to us what you just related. That is, that he decided to strike the Soviets first. Why? Because he knew definitely from his spies and Soviet traitors that the Soviets were going to smash us. He could not afford to wait. It wasn't his fault that the Africans used the C-bomb."

Broward said, slowly, "I never thought of it that way. Perhaps our leaders had planned to crush you Axe. But I doubt it. They knew of Howards' threat to take everybody down with him.

"Anyway, don't you see that it doesn't matter who attacked first? My leaders and yours wanted complete domination. Eventually, despite the menace of the cobalt bombs, the Soviet would have tried for a surprise blow."

"I see," Quiroga replied. "But what can we do about it? We're little men, pawns, helpless pieces in a big game."

"You must know men with authority, men who would like to stop this senseless slaughter?"

Quiroga said, "The commandant of the Deimos garrison. He's a good friend and my cousin on my mother's side. He has stated his sentiments so clearly, however, that I'm afraid he'll be arrested at any moment."

"Do you think he'd listen to me?" said Broward.

Quiroga turned widening eyes to him. " You must be mad? Do you actually think that my cousin would . . . ? It's true he does not believe in this war of extermination. But he is a patriotic man, a brave Argentinean!"

"No, I am not mad. Under ordinary circumstances, I would consider it hopeless to approach him. But I have something with which to bargain. Listen carefully to me, Quiroga. Realize the implications of what I'm about to tell you."

Quiroga listened quietly, but he paled and his face showed horror. Broward finished; Quiroga said, "God! Will you really do *that*?"

"So far, I haven't a choice. I don't want to, but I must to keep your people from doing the same to mine. What do you suggest as a way out?"

"I don't know the recognition code for Deimos. Undoubtedly it has been changed since the last time I was there. But if I made a plea, my cousin might listen, he might allow us to land. However, he probably would think it was a Soviet trick."

"Even if he accepted you and your story, things won't be that simple," Broward said. "I have to guard against a trick, too. I can't place my mission in jeopardy. But we'll give your cousin a try . . . now . . ."

Things were not that simple. Neither were they so complicated, but it did take time to bring them about. Broward altered course to take him far out and then to bring him in again within radarshadow of the moonlet, where the Martian detectors would not find him. Even so, he was open to detection for a long time. At any moment, he expected his equipment to announce the presence of radar or laser beams crossing across his ship or to tell him that it had picked up blips that must be missiles or ships rising from the surface of Mars. He did not expect to see anything coming from Deimos itself, for Quiroga had told him that it had suffered heavily from attack. First, the Soviet missiles had blasted it when the Axe had sprung their attack on Mars. The base on Deimos had expended all its missiles during the repulse. Moreover, its radar and laser external equipment had been wrecked.

New equipment had been brought up from the planet and installed, but Howards would give it no missiles because of a shortage. Then, the South Africans, trapped near this sector, had tried a landing and a storming, the first attack by armed personnel outside a vessel in the history of Mars. Though the South Africans had been killed, they had gained entrance. The price for victory by the Axe was high. Quiroga did not know, but he surmised that the little moon was now being used more as an outpost than anything. He did know that his cousin, Patricio Sullivan y Saavedra, had survived the attack and was commandant—as of the time that the ship, in which Quiroga served, had started out on its mission.

Having determined from the Argentinean that the Deimos base still had some communications equipment, Broward then approached Deimos within two hundred kilometers. It was easy to obtain and maintain the tight-beam contact with Deimos. The moonlet always kept one face toward its primary.

No challenge came from the base. Evidently, the Axe personnel did not want to invite attack; they were playing dead. But, on the side opposite from him, was a beam sending messages to the main base, Osorno, in the area of Eos.

"This is Pablo Quiroga speaking. Commandant Saavedra! Patricio Saavedra! For the love of God, answer! This is Pablo Quiroga, your cousin!"

There was no answer. Quiroga continued to call. Minutes passed. Then, a voice said, "Pablo? What is the matter? What are you doing out there? What is going on?"

Quiroga said, "I am in a lifeboat; I am the only survivor of a battle with a South African fleet. I want permission to land."

Saavedra's voice, with much relief in it, said, "Thanks to Mary, then, that we are out of weapons. Otherwise, I would have had to follow orders and fire on you, even if you were my cousin. That is, unless you had given the proper code, and you could not do that. It has been changed."

"O.K.," Broward said. "Into your suit."

Quiroga got dressed. Broward eased the scout onto a landing circle. This was formed of stone which the Argentineans had smoothed out and filled in. Around it rose the tortured broken peaklets that covered the surface of the tiny satellite. At the base of one of the projections was a metal protrusion, the port for entrance of personnel.

The scout's inner port opened, and Broward said, "Out you go. I'll be waiting to hear from you. But not for long."

The inner port closed; the outer opened. Broward delayed a few seconds to give Quiroga time to get clear before shooting the scout away. In the view plates, he could see the armored figure of the man get smaller, then disappear. Presently, even the landing circle was indistinguishable. The cragged and peaked surface became smooth, and Deimos was a small spindle against the round red-and-bluegreen-and-gray sphere of the mother planet.

Tense, Broward waited. He kept his eyes on the scopes for the first intimations of enemy action from the surface. Now and then, he flicked a look at the moonlet, though he knew that any communication from it would not be visual. What could be going on beneath its rocky cover, in the many hollowed-out rooms and tunnels? Quiroga would have a strange and unconvincing story to tell. For all the commandant knew, there might be a fleet of Soviet vessels nearby. Not that he could believe that very long. Since Quiroga knew the true state of Deimos' defenses, and since he must have been landed by a Soviet, the Soviet must also know that Deimos was defenseless.

In fact, Quiroga's story would be so extraordinary that Saavedra would have no choice but to consider it true. The question was, would he then take the last chance that Mars, and perhaps the human race, had? Or would he attempt to seize Broward?

A half-hour passed. An hour. Deimos and the scout ship kept pace in their hurtling around Mars. Every few seconds, Broward looked at the chronometer on the panel. Fifteen more minutes. If Quiroga had not convinced Saavedra by then, neither of them could stop the death of all life on Mars. He, Broward, would not give them a second past the specified time.

As it was, he had placed his mission in deep peril. But he did have a little hook on which to hang a little hope. That was the fact that Saavedra had not contacted Osorno yet about the Soviet ship. If he had, ships would have appeared on the radarscopes.

Ten minutes. Broward looked at the button that would send the bomb flashing towards the target. It would take the shortest route possible, and it did not care what part of Mars it struck. Any place was as good as any other. It would be traveling so swiftly that it was extremely improbable that an intercept missile could destroy it. So tremendous would its velocity be that, if it had been an ordinary missile or ship, it would have burned up even in the very thin air of Mars. But it was enclosed in a sheath of intertron, a material that would have lasted a long time in the thick atmosphere of Jupiter before melting.

Five minutes. Broward raved and cursed. Did he have to do this because of a man's stupidity or his loyalty to a madman or to a flag? Three minutes. Why wait? Quiroga was probably under arrest. Or was arguing in vain, would argue until doom's day.

Then, the receiver came alive. "Captain Broward! The commandant agrees to talk to you!"

"All right," said Broward, aware that he was sweating and that he was trembling. "We'll do as I said. No tricks now. I'll be on the watch!"

"I give you my word of honor, may Christ strike me dead, if we are planning any treachery."

Broward sent his scout in but not back to the circle. It landed on a ledge of rock which overlooked the port. Should the Argentineans charge out with a mobile laser, they would be cut down by his own beams. Or he could dart off to one side before they could bring it into action and duck behind the peak.

Two men in suits stepped out from the port. They looked around, spotted him, waved, and then leaped into space. Unhampered by the feeble gravity of Deimos, they soared up. Before they had gone far, they were controlling the packs on their back; these sped them straight to the scout. Broward lifted the ship up and back over the peak to take him out of sight and range of the port. A second later, the men rose over its narrow jagged top and landed beside the ship.

After an examination to make sure they carried no weapons, he opened the port. Moreover, he made them abandon the packs outside the craft. And, after they had entered the port and he had shut it, he did not yet open the inner port. Instead, he moved the ship behind another mass of rock. It was possible that the packs, besides containing gravity units, also held small atomic charges. They might be capable of blowing themselves up with the ship or, at least, trying it. Though an explosion ouside the tough metal of the scout probably would not hurt it, it might damage or wreck his sensory equipment.

He shut the outer port and opened the inner just enough so that he could see the two men within.

"Strip off your suits," he said.

"We haven't got anything hidden under them," said Saavedra loudly. Nevertheless, he and Quiroga obeyed. Saavedra was a tall powerfully built man whose handsome face had a family likeness to his cousins. His hair was much darker, but his eyes were blue, and his nose was much bolder.

"I have a gun beside me on this seat," Broward said. "I hope I won't have to use it. I would like it if I never had to use a gun again."

"'There has never been a time in man's history when somebody, somewhere, wasn't using a weapon," Saavedra replied. "But that is no reason for thinking that the future has to be like the past. We are in a situation new to the world."

"You talk like a man I could like," said Broward. "Tell me, what is the situation on Mars?"

"I don't know what use the information will be to you," said the commandant. "But I will do almost anything to keep that bomb—if there is such a bomb—from being delivered. I . . ."

"There is such a bomb. Believe me."

"I can't afford not to believe you. The situation on Mars? It is not what anyone would expect."

Saavedra paused, and Broward said, eagerly, "What do you mean?"

Saavedra took a deep breath, then exploded it. "Rats!"

For a moment, Broward misunderstood him. "Who are rats?"

"Rats. The rats themselves. The rats on Mars."

Broward said that he did not understand.

"There are rats on Mars," Saavedra said slowly. "Rats from Earth. They are in our bases in every conceivable hiding place. And they are thriving in that complex of caverns that exists beneath the base of Osorno. Perhaps you do not know it, but Osorno was built about a tangle of caverns that must run for hundreds of miles under the surface. It was discovered when the base was first established, about twenty years ago. It had an atmosphere, although not as thick as Earth's, of course."

Broward said, "You Argentineans kept quiet about it, but we heard of it. You pumped more air into it, didn't you?"

"Yes. We found the first indigenous life of Mars. Several species of plants that flourished without sunlight. And some very small creatures unlike anything on Earth. Blind and brainless.

"Anyway, the rats that stowed away on the ships, though how they did it, I don't know, adapted there and bred mightily. We have known for some time about them; occasionally, we found one in Osorno. Not only there but the other bases, too, though how they traveled to there is another mystery."

"There were some rats on the Chinese base," Broward said. "But these were exterminated. I believe that rats have journeyed across space with us because they are like us in many ways. Intelligent, highly adaptable, omnivorous, curious, and vicious."

"Perhaps so," said Saavedra. "In any event, they did not constitute a direct threat. But something happened to them back in the caverns below Osorno. They must have caught and eaten the little creatures that thrive there. And, in so doing, must have been bitten now and then and become infected with a disease that afflicts the creatures. This was a mild sickness among the animals of Mars, but, in the bloodstream of the rats, the microbes mutated.

"That is the theory of our scientists. The first we knew of it, we found a few dying rats in our store-rooms and occasionally in the corridors. Then, a man became sick with an undiagnosable malady. He had intense headaches and backaches, his kidneys felt as if they were on fire, he vomited, he alternately suffered from high fevers and raging chills. His tearducts became inflamed, and he wept.

"When the second man fell sick, we named the disease *el fuego de lágrimas*—the 'fire of tears.' Since the rats were suspected, we made a campaign to exterminate them. We killed thousands, but I doubt we got all of them. They are such cunning creatures; they want so hard to live. By that time, one man was spreading the sickness to another. It appeared in all the bases. I think that the disease grows slowly, that many must have been infected before the violent symptoms became present."

"Is it fatal?"

"One person out of twenty has died so far," replied Saavedra. "And the rest are immobilized. Those who have recovered are very weak. It is true that two people out of ten do not seem to be affected. But these are very busy and overworked taking care of the sick."

"Then Mars is prostrate?"

"As if the hand of God had struck," said Quiroga.

"Why should He strike us?" said Saavedra angrily. "We are not atheists. If He wished to strike anybody, it would be the godless Soviets."

"I would say that He—if He did it—has struck mostly at Earth," replied Broward. "And He hasn't spared the Soviets on the Moon, either, although He did his damage by causing them to slay each other. That is, if He thought it necessary to intervene."

"So far, the disease has not appeared on Deimos," said Saavedra. He crossed himself. "May God spare us here!"

"How many personnel do you have here?"

"Ten. The Soviet and South African attacks took many. And after the sickness, all but ten were transferred back to Mars."

"Has Quiroga told you of my offer?"

"Yes. I thought he was mad, but he convinced me. Rather, the fact that you saved his life when you did not have to and that you had no need to ask for help to carry out your mission, convinced me. You must hate your leader and the ideology of the Soviets as much as I hate that madman, Howards, and his anti-Christian policies."

Broward's eyebrows rose.

Saavedra said, "Yes, Howards has always posed as a Christian. But he has cooperated with the Church only when it suited him. Where the Church resisted, Howards has always managed to get rid of the opposition. Of course, always in a subtle or underhanded manner. But my brother, a priest, was one of those who were killed—accidentally— when he spoke out against Howards' confinement of the Pope to his house."

"You are ready to go ahead?" asked Broward.

"It seems to be our only salvation. But what guarantee do I have that your commander will not enslave or kill us?"

"No more guarantee than I have that you will not betray me," said Broward. "But I plan to get rid of my chief just as you plan to get rid of yours. To do that, I may need your help. First, will you swear on your honor and to your God?"

"I will swear. I do swear."

"Then here is what we must do."

Several hours later, the scout returned the two Argentineans to the port. Broward then lifted the little ship from the moonlet and hurled it at top speed towards the area to which the navigational computer directed it. This took an hour and a half. Then, automatically, the radio broadcast the pretaped code call.

For the minutes that it took the waves to get to the area where a robot relay vessel should be located, Broward chafed. Then, he became even more impatient while counting the minutes it would take for the waves to travel back to his ship with the message that the code had been detected, amplified, and was being sent on to the vessel supposedly waiting near the Moon.

Since Broward had arrived in the neighborhood of Mars, Earth had slid around the great curve of the sun and was barred from straight-line communication with the red planet. But the relay ship had been following Broward—he hoped—and had established a position where it could receive and transmit messages both from the scout ship and the Moon.

On schedule, Broward's receiver came to life. His call had been picked up and was sent on its way. Broward, not wanting to wait any longer, then gave his report in the code-form he had prepared on the flight out. This would be passed on, and Scone could digest it, then ask his questions.

The slow torturing moments twisted him. What if there was no one on the Moon to receive? Or what if the Axe had triumphed and were now trying to decipher the code?

"Broward!" Scone's voice said, speaking in English.

Broward almost whooped with joy. The fact that Scone was not using code indicated that the menace of the Axe fleet no longer existed.

"Broward! We received your report. So Mars is dead! Well done. But are you sure that the bomb did the damage it was supposed to? You said that you had delivered the bomb and that it had created the expected havoc in Mars' crust and that the bases on the surface appear to be destroyed. But what about any ships that the Axe might have had in flight at the time the bomb struck? What about Deimos and Phobos? Are they still occupied by the enemy?

"You will investigate them first. Then, you will land on Mars and examine the base of Osorno. Afterwards, return to a point where you can contact the relay and send us a report. We must make sure.

"Meanwhile, for your information, we have utterly defeated the Axe armada. All ships were put out of commission except for two destroyers. These eluded us and are probably on the way back to Mars. Watch for them. If you sight them, avoid them. Note in what direction they are proceeding. As long as they exist, we cannot breathe easily. We suffered heavy losses in gaining victory. Do you hear me?"

"I hear you," replied Broward. "But, before I return to Mars, I would like to speak to my wife. She is all right, isn't she?"

The almost intolerable waiting period passed. Scone's voice sounded again, "Broward! I do not like your disobeying my orders. But, in this great moment of triumph, I am inclined to overlook it. Especially since you did carry out the mission on which so much depended.

"Unfortunately, you cannot talk to your wife.

"Or to mine.

"What do I mean by this? Just this. You may or may not know that it is now the law that every man is to have a mate, even if this means that one woman must have two or more to ensure this. So, I told Ingrid Nashdoi that she must share you with me. She refused and is, therefore, now under arrest. I am sure that she will change her mind later on. She is just having difficulty adjusting to the new ways inevitable because of the conditions. Once she gets over her irrationality and sees the logic of the law, she will agree.

"Perhaps, you would like to speak to her and try to get her to see reason?"

For at least a minute Broward was speechless, his gaze fixed on the speaker as if he could not believe what had come from it. Then, his face a bright red, he roared out obscenities and threats. The veins on his neck were purple columns. He shook his fist, he dredged up every foul name he could think of, and he also told Scone his true sentiments about Scone's methods and philosophies.

But he did not tell Scone what he planned to do on Mars.

Breathing harshly, tears running from his eyes, he finally quit his tirade. He did not wait for a reply from Scone because he had little doubt of what it would be. From now on, as far as he was concerned, Scone had another war on his hands.

Later, after he had cooled down somewhat, he realized that he had reacted exactly as Scone wished. Again, the crafty tiger of a man had killed two birds with one stone— a mixed metaphor that happened to be true. He had gotten Broward to carry out a mission for him and then gotten rid of him. He had placed Ingrid in a position in which, by rejecting Scone, she was breaking a vital law. And he had used this very fact to drive Broward to open rebellion. Thus, he hoped that, when Ingrid had given up hope of seeing Broward again, she would decide to accept Scone.

After all, wasn't Scone now on a footing equal with the greatest of conquerors and emperors of the past? He was the leader of at least 90% of humanity, and he ruled with a direct and powerful fist.

That was not quite true, Broward told himself. In the first place, Scone had several times only killed one of the birds, even if he had thought he was getting both. It was true that Broward had returned from Earth with the bomb, but Moshe Yamanuchi was alive and had an excellent future. Moreover, the Mars question was not settled, far from it.

Perhaps, Scone was not as clever as he thought himself to be.

Thus, Broward found moments of consolation, although these alternated with worries over what would happen to Ingrid and with rage at Scone. Deimos came into view, and he was too busy from then on to think much about Scone or Ingrid.

As he had planned, he took the scout to the bottom of a very narrow crevasse. This was on the side that faced Mars. While the menacing orb hung above him, seeming to be falling towards him, he worked with the tapes. Finally, having checked his instructions, he put on his spacesuit and left the ship. The port closed after him, and he tested the effectiveness of his orders by pointing a pencil-sized emitter at it. The coded frequencies were accepted; the port swung open.

Broward then lifted himself by means of his gravpak from the fissure and shot over the nightmarish surface towards his destination. He was not worried about locating the ship again. When he wished to retrace his way, he would circle the moonlet at a distance far enough away so he could send a radio signal with the pencil-transmitter and be assured that it would cover the area. The ship, on detecting the signal, would rise up from the crevasse until it was within sight.

Outside the port at which he had left the two Argentineans, Broward pressed the activation button. The port opened, and he stepped inside. Quiroga and Saavedra, clad in their service uniforms, were waiting for him.

"I am happy that you returned," said Saavedra. "Frankly, I had my doubts . . ."

"Are things ready for us to take off?" Broward asked.

He walked down the corridor with the two while Saavedra talked.

"Events are working out even better than I had hoped. Almost as if somebody were helping us. Shortly after you left, we received a message from Osorno. A supply boat was coming; this we expected. But we are to send half our personnel back to Mars to help take care of the sick or to replace those who have become sick. So, we won't have to think of an excuse to get down to Mars."

"Did my idea to substitute me for one of your men work?"

Saavedra laughed and said, "So far. I sent my cousin and an electronic maintenance man to a remote sector with orders to repair some equipment there. Pablo knocked him out and locked him up in a room with food and water. But he took off the poor fellow's uniform and identification tags and cards. They're waiting in another room right now. Pablo will bandage your face."

They walked down several corridors, then Quiroga and Broward went into an empty barracks while Saavedra continued. Here, the Moonman took off his garments and replaced them with those of Juan Pedro Malory. Since the commandant had been thoughtful enough to pick a victim Broward's size, the uniform fitted him almost exactly.

"A little tight around the chest," said Broward. "But it'll do."

Quiroga picked up some bandages. Broward sat down in a chair and allowed the young man to wrap the windings around his face. When the job was done, Broward's face was entirely covered except for the eyes.

"You are supposed to have had an accident while repairing the equipment."

Broward grunted and said, "I know. It was my idea."

"Pardon me. I am talking from nervousness. It helps. But listen. The men going with us will be told beforehand about you, Malory, rather. During the trip, you lie down and pretend to be sick. If anyone asks you anything, just groan. Or mumble a little. Your Spanish is intelligible and fluent, but your accent would give you away as a foreigner."

"What about when we get to Osorno? Will we have any trouble contacting this General Mier you spoke of?"

"I hope not."

Saavedra entered the room. "You hope not what?"

Quiroga told him, and the colonel said, "He is the only man with enough power to help us."

"I hope so, too," said Broward, speaking in Spanish. "I may as well tell you that we have," and he glanced at his wristwatch, "twenty-four hours. If we are not back here by then, we will all be dead within a short time after that."

Saavedra walked up to Broward and seized his wrist.

"What are you doing?" said Broward. He started to rise.

"I am not attacking you," answered Saavedra. "Give me your watch. There is none like it among us. You do not want anybody to question you about it, do you?"

"Thanks for noticing it. No, I do not. But didn't you hear what I said?"

"Yes. What do you mean?" answered Saavedra.

"At the end of that time, the ship will automatically leave its hiding place and start on its mission to deliver the bomb."

"*Dios mio*! Why did you arrange that?"

Broward smiled grimly. "I owe my people that much. Also, I wanted insurance that you would carry out your bargain. By the way, don't send men out to look for it while we're gone. Its receptors are active. If anybody but me approaches it, it will take off by itself. And even I will not then be able to find it."

Stiffly, Saavedra said, "I gave you my word."

Broward shrugged and said, "Ordinarily, that would be enough, I assure you. But there is too much at stake. Shall we go?"

The colonel nodded, and they walked to his office. Here, the duffel bag of Malory was waiting. Broward picked it up, noticing the curious stares from a sergeant who accompanied them. The soldier, however, said nothing. Their arrival at the exit port was timed by the colonel to coincide with the landing of the supply boat. He did not want the other men who were to accompany them to get too close a look at Broward. After all, some of those who knew Malory well might notice a difference in Broward's walk or stance. These identified a man as much as anything.

There was an unavoidable delay. The officer commanding the supply ship had to report to the colonel. The cargo had to be unloaded. Saavedra had to sign various reports that he had received all the goods listed. He did this quickly, so quickly that the supply officer made a joke about Saavedra's former thorough and time-consuming check of incoming materials.

"Perhaps you want to get rid of us swiftly so that you will not catch the fire of tears."

"That is not likely," replied the colonel coldly. "I am returning with you to the source of infection."

The officer's jaw dropped. He said, "Back there? I did not know you had orders to go back. Who relieves you?"

"That is none of your business, but I will tell you. I have appointed a lieutenant to take charge. I am needed at Osorno. That should be enough for you."

The officer reddened, but he said nothing more except in the line of duty.

On the supply ship, Broward followed Quiroga and Saavedra to a small cabin near the center of the ship. If anybody thought it was strange that an enlisted man should sit with officers, they said nothing. Thereafter, there was little chance for anything to be noticed. The flight officer came through to check that all passengers were in the stasis areas. A few minutes later, the take-off buzzer sounded. The pilot gave a few instructions and warnings, and they were off towards Mars. Twenty minutes later, they were in the landing port of Osorno.

Saavedra said, "Follow me. I will handle everything." He looked at his wristwatch and shook his head. Like the other two, he could not keep his mind off the ship waiting for automatic instructions at a certain time. Every second was a step closer to doom's day.

Broward's heart was beating hard at this intimacy with so many of the enemy. At the same time, he was curious. He had always wanted to know what the great base of Osorno looked like. This admission port, for instance, was enormous. It had at least fifty separate entrances for ships. After one had entered, air and heat were pumped into the individual port. The men left the vessel and went up a wide ramp into a long stone corridor. This led to a room at least five hundred meters wide and fifty high. There were desks spaced around it, but only a few were manned. At the nearest, the arrivees from Deimos reported in.

The sergeant on duty, a man who looked as if he had been very sick not too long ago, said, "This is Lieutenant Quiroga? He is the man who is the only survivor of the *de Rosas?* He is to report at once to Naval Intelligence."

"My cousin sent in a report," muttered Quiroga to Broward. "Evidently, they want to talk to me in person."

The sergeant gave Broward and his bandaged face a hard look, but Saavedra said, "He burned his face in an accident."

"Then, if I were he, I'd be careful," replied the sergeant. "Those with burns are very susceptible to the sickness of tears. He should report to Hospital Unit No. 10 at once."

"I will see that Quiroga and Malory follow their orders," the colonel said.

He beckoned the two to follow him, and they fell in line. Saavedra walked very swiftly out of the large chamber and down a long high-ceilinged corridor until he came to an elevator. Broward was carrying both his bag and the colonel's suitcase, but, in Mars' weak gravity, they were not heavy burdens. Inside the elevator, the colonel ordered two enlisted men who had just preceded them to leave.

"Take the next elevator. We are on very important business."

The two soldiers left without protest. Saavedra punched the button; the doors closed.

"Get those bandages off while we're going down," the colonel said. "Pablo, help him. It is unfortunate that you were to go to Intelligence, because they may wonder where you are and start investigating. On the other hand, they may not receive word that you are here for a long time or ever. It depends on our luck and on the intentions of God."

Broward stuffed the bandages into his bag just as the elevator stopped. He walked out behind the others into an enormous square room—too big to be called a room, a cavern almost—cut out of granite. Luminescent panels, as on the moon, furnished lighting. Along the farther wall were several buildings composed of blocks of some red material.

"A school and the residences of the teachers," said Saavedra, pointing at some small children playing on swings.

"The blocks are made of *piedras de aire.*"

"What we call foamstone," said Broward. "We've some on the Moon, too."

The colonel glanced again at his watch. "Normally, we could walk through the halls and plazas unnoticed. But so many are sick that anybody traveling around on his own two feet is conspicuous. Nevertheless, we'll have to approach General Mier's office as if we had business there."

Broward wondered if the only way to get anywhere was to use shank's mare. At that moment, a small vehicle rolled out of a corridor into the big chamber or plaza. It was only a lightweight frame on which were mounted the electric fuel-cell-powered motor and four bucket seats. The motor drove the two front wheels and also acted as braking power.

Saavedra hailed the driver, who was a public taxi operator. And, as the driver told them, chattering a Spanish so provincial that the two Argentineans, let alone Broward, had trouble understanding him, he was the only taximan left in Osorno. The others had either been drafted into the hospital services or were themselves too sick to work.

The colonel gave him an address, not correct but near their destination. After going down several different corridors and, once, down a winding ramp into a lower level, the taxi stopped. Saavedra signed a credit chit, and the taxi rolled silently away. The three walked by several barracks, all seemingly empty, and then halted before a three-story foam-stone building at the front of which hung the flag of Argentina.

"In case Intelligence is looking for three men," said Saavedra, "it is better that only one of us go in to make inquiries. Naturally, I will have to talk to the general, since I am the only one who can claim to be his friend. If all goes well, I will send for you."

He was gone for only a minute and returned looking worried.

"There was only one man on duty inside, a corporal. He told me that Mier is sick in his quarters. Mier's wife died, may God receive her soul. She was a gentle woman, a fine lady, the mother of three strong sons and one beautiful daughter."

Broward suggested that, rather than walk or wait for the taxi to come back this way, they commandeer one of the military jeeps parked nearby. No sooner said than done. There was no key problem, since these vehicles had none. Apparently, it had not occurred to the authorities that anybody would steal them in this small and close-knit community. Or maybe the penalties for theft were so severe that crime was scarce.

Two minutes later, they had turned into the largest "plaza" yet and parked before one of the ubiquitous foamstone cubes. The colonel knocked on the door of the ground-floor apartment. Nobody answered; he pushed open the door. The first room was luxuriously furnished by Moon standards; it was filled with furniture of the late nineteenth-century period that must have been imported from Mier's estate in Argentina.

"General! Are you home? It is Colonel Saavedra."

A weak voice bade them come into the bedroom. They went through a large dining-room and down a hallway to the room from which the voice had come.

Mier was lying in bed. He was a dark-skinned man of about fifty-five, bald, and with a craggy face and eagle's-beak nose. He would have been an impressive man at another time. Now, he was shaking and his teeth were chattering. Tears ran down his cheeks.

"General Mier!" Saavedra said. "Have you no one to take care of you? Where is your daughter, your sons?"

"Two of my sons are dead," the general said. "My daughter has gone where only God and the devil know. Rather, the devil knows, for I think she has been made one of Howards' secretaries."

"*Nombre de Dios!* You mean . . . ?"

Mier nodded and then could not stop nodding. Finally, managing to control himself, he said, "When Carlota was ordered to report to that fiend, I knew what was in store for her. I phoned Howards, begged that she be allowed to remain with me, to nurse me. But he refused. He said the state needed her. The state! *L'état, c'est* Howards! Carlota is a beautiful girl, and that beast saw her and desired her. He dared to take her only because I am sick and he thinks I will die soon.

"Oh, if only my son, the only left alive to me, my brave strong Ulises, were here! He would do what I am too weak to do. He would avenge our honor."

"We will avenge you," cried Saavedra. "But it would be senseless to try to storm Howards' building with only three of us. We would accomplish nothing but our own deaths."

"If I could walk, if I could hold a gun," Mier said, "I would go into that building alone. I would shoot until they killed me. At least, I would have shown them that the father of Carlota Mier is no coward nor a man to treat lightly."

"No one doubts your courage," the colonel said. "But we are here for something even more important—if you will forgive me for saying so—than removing the stain on your family honor. We are here to save Mars. To save humanity."

"I do not understand," Mier replied through clicking teeth.

Saavedra told him as swiftly as he could, touching only the most significant of the events that had brought them here.

Mier said, "Holy Mother of Christ! My Ulises was with the fleet that was sent to the Moon! Young man, you *yanqui*, you say that two of our ships did escape? Destroyers?"

"That is right."

Mier raised himself a little from his pillows, but he fell back. "Then there is still a chance that my Ulises is alive. He was on a destroyer."

"Let us hope so," Broward answered. "And, if our plans work, your son may live to be a hundred or more. And you may have many fine grandchildren."

Mier said, "There is only one thing to do. My friends, those who have been wronged by Howards, those who hate him only because of what he is, these must help us."

Saavedra suggested several names. At each one, Mier shook his head.

No. That one was dead. No. That one was on Phobos. No. This one was even sicker than he, Mier. That one was no man; he had been greatly wronged but he loved his worthless life more than his self-respect.

Again, Saavedra looked at his wristwatch. "Is there no one to help us? Surely . . ."

"There is His Holiness," Mier said.

"But he is a priest," Saavedra replied. "What could he do?"

"Wait a minute," Broward said. "The Pope escaped? He is here?"

"Not the saintly Pelagio III," said Quiroga. "He was in Buenos Aires when the bombs struck. The present Holy Father was Father Vonheyder, the Bishop of Mars. He assumed the pontificate, as was his right, and the name of Siricio II. Saint Siricius, his namesake, was the 38th pope."

"We've no time for ecclesiastical history," the colonel said. "I will admit that the Holy Father has reason to wish that another than Howards was his secular chief. It is obvious by now to everyone that Howards would like for all of the remaining priests in the world to die. There are only thirty left. But he would not dare to make an overt move against them. He would have a revolt on his hands."

Broward said, suddenly, "There's your answer!"

Startled, they stared at him. "What do you mean?"

"Look, I know you aren't going to like what I'm about to propose. But a desperate situation requires swift and desperate measures. You can't afford to be scrupulous. What if one of you made an anonymous call to Howards? Told him that the Pope was plotting to lead a revolt against him because the Pope fears that the Church is in mortal danger of perishing forever?

"Then Howards will be forced to arrest Siricio. And when that happens, you can get some quick action and support from those who have hitherto held back. They won't dare not fight; their souls will be in danger if they do."

Saavedra exploded. "You are crazy, you atheist Soviet! We should betray the Holy Father to save our lives? And lose our souls?"

"I would not think of it" Quiroga said. His face was white. Mier's weakening voice seemed to originate at the bottom

of his lungs and taper off before it reached his lips. Broward
went over him.

"Do not try to force the Holy Father into such a situation.
He will not be your tool. But go to him, talk to him. Perhaps he can suggest something. He is a very wise and a very
strong man. And there are many devout Catholics here.
Originally, Howards sent high-ranking potential trouble-makers here, many of whom were Catholics, to get rid of
them. But that was before he thought of coming here himself.
The Holy Father was one of those he got transferred to Mars.
Talk to him. Perhaps . . ."

Saavedra said, "Is he all right?"

"I think he's dying," replied Broward. He moved away to
allow the colonel to get closer to Mier. But Mier spoke loudly
enough for all to hear.

"*Ay de mi!* Save my daughter! Save . . ."

There was a rattling. The general's mouth dropped open,
and his eyes stared.

Saavedra covered the face with a sheet. He was weeping. "He was my friend!" he sobbed. "He was a brave
man!"

Quiroga had already picked up a phone and was trying to
get through to a priest. But Broward pressed the button
that turned the phone off.

"We'll go to the Pope's house," he said. "We can send a
priest from there to Mier. There's no time to waste."

"We will be under surveillance," said Saavedra. "The
moment we enter, Intelligence will know. It won't be difficult
for them to identify Pablo and me. And a little checking will
tell them that we left the port with a third man whose face
was bandaged. That will be enough for them to investigate.
They won't lose any time."

"What do you suggest? We haven't any time to lose, either."

The two Argentineans looked helpless. Broward said, "I'm
going there. Don't stop me. You know what will happen if you
do."

Saavedra took a handkerchief from his pocket and wiped
his eyes. He said, "Very well. We'll go with you. God help
us, we can do nothing else."

On the way, Saavedra said, "So far, we've been lucky not to
have been stopped by roving *Angelos*. These Angels are
Howards' personal army and secret service. They have many
privileges, which they abuse. One of them is the right to stop

and question any citizen whom they think suspicious. They do it quite frequently and use the opportunity to get bribes."

They drove through various corridors of varying sizes. At the intersections of the tunnels were signs, suspended from the ceilings, that indicated the names and east-west or north-south locations and the levels. Saavedra was familiar with this section, so he did not have to use the maps in the jeep. But he confessed that there were many parts of Osorno where he would have been lost without their help.

"When this city—if this city—expands through the rest of the cavern complex, plus the additional hollowing-out to be done, it will have a population of two million. But another complex, even larger than this one, has been discovered only a hundred kilometers away. When the two are linked up and colonized, the population will be larger than that of Buenos Aires was."

The jeep halted before a line of elevator doors. The colonel pressed a button on the panel of the jeep, and the door directly in front of them slid open. The jeep entered; Quiroga got out to press the down button.

"If Osorno grows to be a great city," Broward said, "it will be haunted by the thought that some day another bomb, such as the one now above Mars, may be dropped on this planet. If we succeed here, I intend to destroy the bomb that now exists. But the people who made it, they still exist, and they can make another. If they survive under the sea and some day emerge, they will be a threat to all of humanity."

The elevator stopped, the door opened, the jeep drove out onto the third level.

"Destroy the bomb by dropping it on Earth," said Saavedra. "That way, you will kill two birds with one stone. The bomb and knowledge of how to make it will cease to exist in a single explosion."

"I cannot do it. How can I know for sure that another bomb will be made or that it'll be used? Besides, I am sure that there are other places under the ground and under the seas of Earth where others, innocents, you might say, live. They, too, would die."

"Man has always lived under some form of threat of annihilation," Quiroga said. "In the ancient times, it was the wrath of God or plague and then it was the atomic bombs; somehow, he has managed to survive."

"His luck may run out at any minute," Broward replied. "Oh, oh, who are they?"

They had left the elevator chamber and driven through a long tunnel into a tremendous plaza. Now, a jeep with three men was driving towards them, and its siren was whooping. Two of the three men were armed with submachine guns.

"The Angels," said Colonel Saavedra. "You will notice that traffic is very small here. It always is. That neo-Gothic building over there is Howards' residence. Anybody who enters this plaza is likely to be challenged. He takes no chances."

"If they try to take us into custody, shoot," Broward said. He nodded at another building across the plaza from Howards' mansion. By the colonel's descrption, he knew it was the Pope's house. "We'll make a run for it."

"Then what?" muttered Quiroga.

Broward stopped the jeep. The Angels' vehicle turned broadside and halted just before the jeep. Its occupants, dressed in white uniforms with much gold braiding, got out. One of the gunners walked around behind the jeep to cover it. The officer approached from the driver's, Broward's, side. The second gunner remained by his car.

The officer, a short very muscular man with a hard face, said, "Let's see your identification and travel permits."

"We just got here from Deimos," the colonel replied. "I was told nothing about local travel permits."

"Your identification," said the officer harshly.

Broward reached into his coveralls, saying, "I have the permit, Captain. I did not think it necessary to burden the colonel with knowledge of it."

His words did not make logic, but he was talking to divert the officer's mind. The captain reached out his hand to take the papers, and Broward pressed the little knob on the matchbox-sized object in his hand. The captain, his heart muscles spasming, fell to the ground.

Broward whirled around and caught the other two with a sweep of the beam. The man by the jeep fell at once. The other, behind the jeep, shifted the tommy to his shoulder to fire, and then he fell face forward on his weapon.

"Knock them out," ordered Broward loudly. "Quickly. They'll recover almost at once."

He jumped from the jeep and brought the edge of his palm against the thick neck of the captain, who was just rising from the ground. As if it had been planned, the colonel took the man nearest him, the Angel by the official vehicle. He drove his knee upwards to catch the rising man under the chin with it. The Angel fell backwards and struck the back of his neck against the wheel. Quiroga kicked the gunner behind the jeep in the belly.

Broward looked across the plaza towards Howards' building. The plaza was empty, and nobody was coming out of the mansion. It seemed incredible that nobody had noticed the fight. But they had not.

Under Broward's direction, the Angels were dragged into the back of the jeep. "Quiroga, drive their jeep into the corridor. I'll drive ours there."

In the corridor, out of sight of anybody in the plaza, Broward began to undress the captain. The others followed suit with each of the Angels.

"What do we do with them?" said the colonel. He glanced toward the tunnel leading to the elevator chamber.

"Why didn't I think of that?" moaned Broward. "Let's get out of here and into an elevator. We'll do the uniform exchange there."

They drove the jeeps into the tunnel and thence into the room beyond and then dragged the unconscious men into the elevator at the extreme left end of the room. Quiroga started it downward, then resumed taking his man's clothes off. He paused several times to reverse the elevator's direction.

"That little weapon of yours is a wonderful device," the colonel said. He was breathing hard. "We don't have anything like that, that I know of."

"It's comparatively new," Broward replied. "But it's only effective at short range, and the attack only lasts as long as the beam is directed against the victim. Moreover, it takes a lot of energy. I have about one charge left in it—I think."

They completed the switch. One Angel groaned, and Broward kicked him hard in the head. "Stop it at the level where we got on," he said to the lieutenant. "We've got to get something to hold the door open while we send this elevator back up again. We'll drop these men down the shaft."

The cage stopped; the door slid open. With the tommy held ready, Broward stepped out into the room. He saw five Angels getting out of a jeep; the foremost was walking towards another elevator entrance.

He could not take a chance that they would stop him to talk. He sprayed the group with one burst.

The chamber rang with noise as loud as doom. Then, there was silence.

"Now you've done it," the colonel said. "They'll come running from everywhere."

"Maybe the noise didn't reach them," Broward said. "Anyway, I had no choice. Come on. Let's get rid of them."

He removed his knife from its sheath beneath his coveralls and stabbed each of the three original Angels in the solar plexus. Then, reopening the elevator door, he shoved one of the bodies in to keep the door from closing while the cage ascended. Quiroga shoved the door open even further, and Broward and Saavedra placed another body beside the first to enlarge the opening. Fortunately, the mechanism had no safety provision which kept the cage from moving while the door was not shut. There were no cables attached to the cages, which operated off self-contained gravitypaks.

The bodies, shoved through the opening over the corpses used as doorstops, fell unimpeded to the bottom. When these had been disposed of Broward and Saavedra used jackets stripped from the dead men to wipe away as much of the blood as possible. Unfortunately there was nothing they could do about the scratches on the doors or the chips in the stone walls left by ricocheting bullets. Quiroga placed the weapons of the fallen on the floor of their jeep.

Broward drove that vehicle, and the other two were driven by the colonel and the lieutenant. They went back down the corridor and then swung to the side of the plaza on which was the Pope's residence. Broward was relieved that there were no people to be seen. But he knew that they could be easily viewed from within the buildings. As if he had official business, he steered the jeep to the pontiff's building and then around to its rear.

He had to knock hard about twenty times before the back door swung in. A young man in black robes and with an expressionless face confronted him.

"We must see His Holiness at once," the colonel said.

"You may wait inside for him," the priest replied firmly. "The Holy Father is holding a private conference now. He is not to be disturbed."

Broward considered telling him that they were not Angels. But there was the possibility that Howards had succeeded in planting a spy in the Pope's household. Perhaps, it might be this man.

"El Macho sent us," he said. "We have orders to see His Holiness at once."

The priest did not answer; he seemed not to know what to do. Or else he was shocked by the fear that Howards had finally decided to move against the Church.

Broward shouldered him aside, and Saavedra and Quiroga followed.

The priest grabbed hold of Broward's arm and said, "You must not do this. It would be a mortal sin; your souls will be in jeopardy."

No spy would act thus. Broward said, "We are not what we seem. We are not Angels, despite these uniforms. Now, do you understand? We must see His Holiness at once. The fate of all life on Mars depends on it."

"Follow me."

They were led through several small rooms, Spartanly furnished, to a hall. At the end of the hall, near the front of the building, was a staircase. Like most on Mars, the steps were much further apart than those of Earth. A man used to handling himself under the lesser gravity could spring easily from one to the next. In fact, if you were in a hurry, you could make it in one jump to the top of the stairs.

The three went up the stairs and then down the hall to its end. Here, the priest knocked on a door. A voice from within said, "What is it?"

"An emergency, Your Holiness," the priest said quietly. "There are three men here who say that the fate of Mars depends upon your seeing them at once."

There was a muttered exclamation. The door opened. The Pope was a tall thin man of about fifty, dressed in ordinary clerical garb. He had a face that would have been handsome if it had not been so haggard. He was very dark and looked like an Indian despite the fact that his patronymic came from a Prussian baron who had emigrated to Argentina in the early twentieth century.

Behind him stood a woman whose face was veiled. She moved forward, and then knelt and kissed his hand. He gave her a blessing; she rose and silently walked out of the room and down the hall. The three looked curiously after her. She had a beautiful figure.

On seeing their uniforms, the Pope's eyes had widened. Now, he said, "Three Angels, heh? I hope that this is a good omen."

He stepped aside. Broward entered first. The other two kissed the pontiff's hand. He said to Broward, "If you are not an Angel nor an angel, then you are not Howards' man. Nor are you a Catholic. What, then, are you?"

He closed the door, signing to the young priest that he was dismissed. Broward said, "Your Holiness, it is unfortunate that it will take a little time to explain. But I ask that you listen to us to the end."

The Pope nodded for him to go ahead. He paced back and forth in the little room while Quiroga and Saavedra stood by the door. Now and then, he asked a question to clear up a point. On hearing that Broward was a Soviet, he reacted only by raising his eyebrows. When Broward had trouble phrasing a particular statement, the pontiff said, "You may speak in English if you wish. I am fluent in all the major languages."

At the end of twenty minutes, Broward had given his history.

"You would not have come here if you could have gotten help elsewhere," the Pope said. "Now, what do you expect, or hope, that I will do?"

"Your Holiness," Broward replied, "if there were any other way to bring about peace, I would take it. But violence is the only way. And . . ."

"Why did you come down here in person?" said the Pope. "Why did you not send these two men down with the message that you would launch the bomb if Mars did not surrender?"

He stopped, then said, "Forgive my stupidity. Howards would not believe you, of course; he would have sent ships after you, and you would have been forced to launch that devil's device. Only by overthrowing the present government could you save Mars."

"That is right," said Broward. "And Howards will not listen to anything but a bullet now."

"The servant should obey his master, so St. Paul said. And our Lord said to render unto Caesar what is Caesar's."

"Do you mean to tell me that you obey your political master even if he is evil and is intent on grinding your Church to bits under his heel? Did not Christ whip the money-changers out of the temple? And haven't there been bishops and priests in the Church's history who went into battle at the sides of their secular lords and slew the heathen?"

"True," said the pontiff. "However . . ."

There was a knock on the door, and the young priest came in.

"Your Holiness, there are armed Angels coming out of Howards' house. They are coming across the plaza towards us. I fear . . ."

"It has happened later than I thought it would," the Pope said. "You must have been seen when you came around the house. Probably, those watching you thought you were here on business because of your uniforms, even if they had not been notified that Angels were to come here.

"But they also have very sensitive sound-receptors trained on this building. Nothing that is said goes unmonitored over there except for my room, which has been especially sound-proofed. And I only got that concession because I threatened to cause trouble, just as I had to suspend confession until I got the confessional booths insulated. Howards had no compunctions about using spy-beams on those."

Broward rushed down the hallway to the window at the end. Halfway across the plaza, advancing slowly, were about twenty men. All were equipped with burpers or rifles except the officers, who wore side-arms. They were spread out in two lines in a crescent, the horns of which enclosed the area beyond both sides of the pontiff's residence.

Broward rolled the window into the slot in the wall, poked the muzzle of his tommy out, and began firing. Within a few seconds, two other tommies also began firing; these were from rooms on both sides of the hall. Quiroga and Saavedra, without waiting for orders from him, had joined the fight.

The Angels in the center who had not been hit raked the front of the house with return fire from their burpers. But Broward, after downing at least six at the first burst, had stepped back from the window. He saw men on the left horn of the crescent run towards the side of the buildings. Three reached safety, but two fell as he shot out of the side of the window.

He ran down the hall to the top of the stairway, paused to jump the length of the steps to the ground floor, but stopped when he heard a burper firing outside in the rear. He ran to the window at the rear of the hall, almost knocking the Pope down, and looked out cautiously.

The young priest was standing behind one of the jeeps and was holding a burper. Obviously, he had been hiding behind the vehicle. Broward decided that it was safe to put his head out of the window. Five bodies were sprawled on the ground along the base of the house.

The Pope, looking out past him, said, "So Father Ignacio took a hand in this without consulting me?"

"I'm sure he did it on impulse," replied Broward. "He

didn't join me; he didn't know why I was here. He was only protecting you."

"As Peter drew his sword and sliced off the servant's ear," said Siricio II. "Well, I am not going to rebuke Ignacio or tell him to put up his weapon."

"You'll fight with us?"

"I'll fight in my way," replied the Pope. "I will not shed blood. But I will march with you. By the way, whatever you are going to do, you had better do it at once. I'm sure that Howards has called soldiers to come to his aid. There is a barracks in the next plaza. However, I doubt that more than a quarter of the soldiers will be able to respond. The rest are too sick."

Broward returned to the front window. Quiroga and Saavedra joined him. An Angel, his white uniform splotched with red, was feebly crawling away.

There was no sign of movement from the building across the way. But Broward was sure that armed men were standing behind the windows there.

"I wish I had some gravpaks," he said.

"We have several in the supply room," said the Pope.

"Four should be enough. Let's get them."

A few minutes later, one pak had been tied to the center left side of a jeep. Manipulating the pak's controls, Broward caused the vehicle to be raised several feet in the air. Then he guided the featherweight until it lay on its side at right angles to his jeep across the front. Father Ignacio supplied the strips, torn from sheets, that anchored the near-weightless frame to the front of Broward's vehicle.

"It'll make a shield," the Moonman said. "If their bullets don't wreck the pak or cut the strips, it'll do fine."

He and the two officers slipped into the harnesses attached to the paks, tightened them, and tried the pak controls. Then, they got into the jeep.

"Father Ignacio will take the other jeep and make a run for the elevators," said the Pope. "He will spread the word on the upper levels that Howards is trying to kill me. It will not be a lie, because I am certain that Howards will take such action when he sees what I am about to do."

"Holy Father, what is that?" cried Saavedra.

"What I should have done long ago but held off doing because of politics, or rather, fear of meddling in politics. Also, I was afraid. I was afraid that the Church might be crushed, and I sinned in thinking that, for the Church will live as long as God decrees, and we know how long that is. Worse, I feared for my sheep. If I denounced Howards and I were imprisoned, who then would protect them from the wolves? I should have known Whom that Person would be."

Broward hesitated. What if the Angels seized the Pope as a hostage? Well, what if they seized anybody as such? That which must be done would be done, no matter who got hurt.

Father Ignacio said, "Holy Father, he will kill you! He is a vile and evil man!"

The Pope held up his hand in remonstration. "Do not try to stop me. I have delayed too long now. Do as I said."

Ignacio dropped to his knees and said, "Father, bless me!"

"And you, young man, bless me. And do not forget to tell the others that, if I do not return, Father Mendoza should succeed me."

The young priest wept. Siricio said, "Compose yourself and come with me. You must hear my confession."

Broward paid them no attention, for he was carefully instructing the other two in the plan of attack. They objected several times, and he answered them. They had some good points which he accepted and thus changed the course of the assault.

By then, Father Ignacio had come back outdoors. With him was another priest, a man about the pontiff's age. Broward was surprised, for he had seen nobody else while he was in the house.

"Father Gomez was at his prayers," said Father Ignacio, as if that explained his nonappearance. "He will go the opposite direction I'll take; he'll try to head off the troops stationed nearby."

Broward wondered why the troops had not appeared if they were so near. The young priest, answering, said, "I'm puzzled. I do not know. But His Holiness wishes to see you."

Broward went into the house just in time to see the pontiff coming out of a room near the front door. He was wearing a small plastic box which hung from a cord around his neck and lay on his chest.

"I want everybody in the plaza to hear my voice," he said. He smiled at Broward. "Tell me, my son, why have you, a Soviet and an atheist, placed your life in jeopardy to save your enemy?"

"I do not believe in the Soviet ideology," Broward said. "As for my so-called atheism, I am not so sure now about it.

I have seen some strange things recently. I mentioned the man Moshe Yamanuchi. But I did not have time to tell you that he felt that Something, a Voice, was urging him."

"Ah, yes, the Jew. God would not allow the Chosen Race to die out. It is not time yet."

"Moshe would not agree with your view of that, I'm sure. But he does agree with you that there is a God. However, you do not have to be a Christian or a Moslem or a Hindu to love mankind, to want to see them happy. I did not want to be a mass murderer. By killing the people of Mars, I drive another nail into Man's coffin. Too many nails have been hammered in lately; a few more, and Man will be buried forever."

"You could not love Man unless you also loved God," replied Siricio. "You may deny it, but I am sure that you do, somewhere in your being."

"Perhaps," Broward replied. "But let's get on with what we have to do. You wanted to talk to Howards and his men first, right? I can give you a minute or two. That is, if the troops don't show. When they do, I have to move."

"Good bye, my son," said the Pope. "I hope I will see you again in a place we both will like."

"I doubt it," said Broward. "But nobody's ever disproved that there is such a place."

"I would not believe them if they did."

He blessed Broward and then stepped out. Broward watched him cross the great plaza, stepping around the corpses, stopping once to examine a man, apparently to determine whether or not he was alive. Broward also glanced at the two entrances to the plaza. Both were still deserted.

The erect and lonely figure of the priest became smaller as he neared the neo-Gothic front of the building. This had its back placed solidly against the rock wall of the huge cavern, and it extended for about 20 meters outwards. The front reared up straight like a cliff carved with the heads of men, gargoyles, animals and various religious and secular symbols. It was the only one of its kind that Broward had seen here, though such buildings were numerous on Earth. There were no steps to the main entrance, which lay flush with the plaza floor. The entrance itself was wide enough for six men to go in shoulder to shoulder and high enough that a man standing on another's shoulders could not reach the top. It had two plastic gates of open grillework.

Behind the gates stood a man in a white uniform. Behind him was a mob of men. At that distance, the face of the man in front was not recognizable, but Broward thought it must be Howards. He had a reputation for not liking to have more than one person at a time near him.

The Pope halted, only a few meters from the gates. Suddenly, a great voice spoke. It bounced off the front of the house and the plaza walls behind it and came as a thunderous echo to Broward.

"Howards! And those who serve Howards! Mars is doomed!"

And the voice told of the ship that waited somewhere above the red planet and of the weapon of total destruction and death that it carried. It told what would happen if Howards was not unseated at once and a new government formed. It went on to describe graphically what would result.

Broward looked at the tunnels. No one yet. Then, he saw a jeep drive along the front of the buildings and cut across at top speed and enter the tunnel that led to the elevators. Father Ignacio was driving it.

So far, so good. No one behind the windows of the president's house had fired at the young priest.

"You are an evil man," the voice boomed. "You, Howards, are guilty of spilling the blood of countless men, women, and children. I am not talking of the murders you had committed on Earth for your vile political purposes. I accuse you of exploding the cobalt bombs on Earth so that all life would perish there. I accuse you of planning to do so to the end that you might then come to Mars and be sole ruler of all mankind. I accuse you of the murder of eight billion people and of all the life that God created to flourish on the face of His green Earth, green no longer.

"I could accuse you of many other evil and monstrous deeds, such as the adultery you are now contemplating forcing on a virtuous wife and the fornication you are now forcing on the daughter of General Mier.

"But these, evil though they may be, are as nothing to the murder of Earth!"

The scream that came from the man by the gates could be heard even across the plaza. The white figure pointed at the Pope, its head turned towards those behind him. Obviously, he was ordering them to fire.

But nobody obeyed. Even these men hesitated.

Then, the white figure pulled a weapon from the white holster on its white belt. There was a spurt of flame which Broward could see because his angle of vision was between the two men on the opposite sides of the gate. Another followed the first, and another.

Siricio II fell backward and lay on the rock floor, his arms spread out.

Broward cast another look at the tunnel but saw no one. Then he turned and sprinted down the hall, burst through the door, and cried, "Let's go!"

Quiroga and Saavedra were sitting in the jeep that had the other jeep placed on its hood. "We heard him," said Quiroga. He was white and shaking. "We heard the shots, too. Was the Holy Father . . . ?"

Broward nodded and climbed into the jeep behind Quiroga, who was in the driver's seat. "Howards murdered him."

"Holy Mother of Mary!" said Saavedra. Both Argentineans crossed themselves.

"Howards' men will be stunned," said Broward. "They can't help it. Let's go!"

Quiroga sat motionless except for the silent moving of his lips. His hands gripped the little wheel on the end of the long flexible steering rod. He stared straight ahead.

Broward pounded him hard on his back. "Are you going to sit here and be slaughtered like the Holy Father?" he shouted. "Come on now! Or get out and let me take your place! I'll do it alone if you've lost your guts!"

Quiroga said, harshly, "I'm all right. And watch your language. No man calls me a coward."

The jeep started slowly around the rear of the house. Then, when it rounded the corner, it straightened out. Quiroga turned the acceleration disc, and the jeep surged ahead so swiftly that all three were thrust back against the seats. Broward picked up one of the burpers from the floor and looked at the upper row of windows in the building. It was from there that the fire of the Angels would be most dangerous. The closer the jeep got to the building, the better angle those in the upper story would have to shoot over the vehicle that was their shield.

"This is going to take good timing," he said to Saavedra, who held a knife in one hand. "When I give the word . . ."

The plaza became a hell of noise. The entire front of the building seemed to blaze. But Broward was already pulling his head down when the hail came and the jeep began to shake. Bullets went whing! zeeee! past them; explosive bullets struck the body of the shield and bent it over towards the men.

Quiroga had locked the controls and slipped from the seat to the hood, unhindered because there was no windshield. Saavedra and Broward, crouching, followed him beneath the shelter of irradiated plastic that formed the vehicle's body.

Broward peered through the opening between the shield and the hood. "Slow it down!" he shouted to Quiroga, who held the controls in his hands. The shaft, capable of being telescoped and very flexible, was bent forwards over the hood.

The jeep checked, and the men slid against the frame of the shield. Broward's head banged into a tire; for a second he almost blacked out.

Then, the three were pressed against the frame; the jeep had rammed into the building. Saavedra slashed at the strips of sheet that held one end, then slid the knife over to Broward. He grabbed at it, it struck his hand, and dived off the hood onto the ground. Without thinking, he jumped off the hood, picked up the knife, and leaped back onto the hood. Explosive bullets, striking the rock floor, threw chips of stone like sharpnel and zinged off the hood.

He felt something sharp hit his face, put his hand up, and it came away with blood. But he used the other hand to slash at the strips holding down his end of the shield. In the meantime, the others, weightless because of their gravpaks, were clinging to the underside of the shield. It rose, pulled upwards by the counterdrive of the paks attached to it. Broward sprang up and grabbed hold of a jeep wheel, his momentum sending the vehicle more quickly upwards.

They floated up the front of the building while bullets poured into the jeep on the building side. Then, the fires ceased. Apparently, or so it seemed to Broward, the solid bullets were ricocheting back through the windows and the explosive bullets were going off too close to the shooters.

Clinging to the underside like a baby Martian spider to its mother, Broward looked down. They were just above the top row of windows. Now, the men should be running out into the plaza to get a shot at them from the exposed side. And the men in the window now below should be leaning out to fire up at them.

"Use your paks!" he screamed. "Up and over!"

They soared above the ascending jeep, corrected their controls, and were on the roof.

Broward had been afraid that men would be up there. If

so, the three would be helpless targets. But there was no one there. Not yet.

He landed, flipped off the pak power, and turned to the others.

Quiroga was all right. Saavedra was not there.

He followed the line indicated by the young officer's pointing finger. Saavedra was still rising towards the ceiling of the cave. His head lolled; blood spurted out of the hole created when his knee had been blown off.

Quiroga crossed himself and then began, with Broward, to look for entrances on the roof to the story below. But there were none.

Broward cursed and then said, "That figures. He wouldn't want an assassin using the same approach as us."

"What do we do?" Quiroga said. "They'll be putting on paks and coming up after us in a minute."

Broward looked up at Saavedra's body, now pressed against the ceiling of the cave, and at the jeep, still rising.

"I'd say we've had it. But we're still alive. Maybe . . ."

Quiroga, who was facing the wall of rock at the rear of the building, shouted and fired his burper. Broward whirled and saw that a section of the rock, just above the juncture of the building and wall, had moved outwards.

He jumped to one side to be out of sight of anyone on the other side of the half-opened door. Quiroga fired another burst and then ran over after Broward. The Moonman stopped by the door, fell to the roof, shoved his gun under the door and into the opening beyond. He squeezed the trigger and did not release it until he had loosed at least thirty explosive bullets, as indicated by the tiny counter on the barrel.

Quiroga leaped through the opening as soon as the shooting stopped. Broward rose, hesitated a moment, then, hearing nothing, went around the rock-door. The lieutenant was standing inside an open half-cage, which, in turn, was in a shaft hollowed out of the rock. The only light came from a lamp mounted on a thin pole on one side of the cage. This was mounted on a gravity-unit.

The cage and the walls of the shaft around it, however, were spattered with blood and covered with gobbets of flesh. The stream of explosive bullets poured in by Broward had literally blown the Angels apart. The head of one was missing; it had been knocked over the cage and down into the shaft or else had disintegrated.

Broward said, "Let's get what's left of them out of here. Lucky for us we didn't destroy the controls."

Part of the plastic rails around the cage had been shattered and there were dents in the floor, but this was the only damage. Before starting to clear out the remains, Broward looked above them and also peered over the edge, for there was some space between the cage and the shaft. Darkness above and below.

"I think that Howards may have prepared this for a secret getaway," he said. "He probably sent these men up to get us from the rear. Maybe nobody else knows."

They dumped the legs and arms and torsos over and kicked bits of flesh and bone down the shaft. Then Broward pulled on the grips fastened to the back of the door and swung it in.

"If the men that'll be coming after us from the outside don't know about this shaft, they're going to be mightily puzzled."

"Yes, but when they report to Howards," Quiroga said, "he'll know soon enough what's happened."

Broward hesitated. Up? Or down? If they descended, they might catch Howards by surprise and kill or capture him. This did not seem very likely. Although Howards did not like many people close to him, he made sure that his bodyguards were not too far off. Still, it might be worth taking a chance. The only drawback was that, even if they did get to Howards, they would surely be killed afterwards. Then, the bomb would come.

Besides, he was very curious about where the upper part of the shaft led.

Either way, he had to do something fast. It was possible that Howards might be able to cut off the power to the cage by remote control.

He tested the button marked with an arrow pointing upward, and the cage began moving up. There was a little wheel by the two buttons; he turned it to the right and the cage picked up speed. Rotating the wheel to the left slowed it down until it was crawling. The button marked A (for *alto*, "halt" he supposed) stopped the cage.

Having mastered the controls, he resumed upward progress at full speed. Quiroga turned the lamp, which was on a joint, so that it shone straight above them. A minute passed, and Quiroga said, "I think we've passed the second level." A few seconds later, he said, "We should be about even with the top of the first level. Do you think this goes to the surface?"

"We'll find out soon enough. There's the end of the shaft."

They rose to the opening. Before reaching it, the cage had begun to slow down without operation of the controls. It stopped, and the two men got off.

They were in a well-lighted place, one large enough to hold several of the type of the four-seater spaceship that it did contain. The chamber was hollowed out of granite and, beside the craft, had several cots, a tank of water, a large box full of provisions, canned food, medical supplies, and liquor. The illumination came from several mobile luminescent panels leaning against the walls.

The ship's port was open. Broward stepped inside; Quiroga followed.

"You know how to handle the controls?" the Moonman said. "They're unfamiliar to me."

The lieutenant examined the control panel, shook his head, and said, "This one can't be activated unless you have the key. Guess who has that."

"Can't you rewire it? Or isn't there time?"

"Even if there were, I wouldn't try it," Quiroga said. "I imagine that Howards has this rigged to explode if anybody tampers much with it."

"I don't know. He wouldn't think anybody would have access to it. Which reminds me. How do you get out of here?"

They examined the walls. Undoubtedly, some section of it must open to an air-lock and beyond that to the surface. The rock around them must be part of a hill or cliff, and it must be out of sight of the domes above Osorno. But there was nothing within to indicate the exit. No slightest crack.

"It's probable," said Quiroga, "that Howards must activate the mechanisms that open this with a radio or laser frequency. He might carry the emitter with him, or it might be part of the ship. More likely the latter, since he could open this from the surface easier if the emitter were built into the ship."

"So," said Broward, "we're where we were before. Meanwhile, Howards must have found out what happened on the rooftop. We can expect some sort of a move against us at any moment."

He went from the control cabin into the rear. There was a tiny washroom, spaces in the corridor for bunks, and, beyond, a storage room. At the rear wall of this, he opened a door and looked into the compartment containing the motor, generator, fuelpile, and electronic equipment. There was also a box that looked like a tool box.

Gingerly, for he feared booby-traps, he stepped through the door and then snapped up the catch that held the cover. A minute later, he was back in the control cabin with a hammer, several screwdrivers, pliers, tape, and two cold chisels.

Quiroga said, "You know that we'll probably set off an alarm or some kind of booby trap."

Broward shrugged. "Too bad. But there's nothing else to do."

"You get outside the ship," the Argentinean said. "I'm expendable. But if you die, everybody dies."

"One man only'll take too much time. Come on. No argument now."

"No," Quiroga said firmly. "Somebody has to guard the shaft. They'll be coming up with gravpaks and quickly."

"All right," said Broward. He turned and walked out of the ship to the elevator. He got on the cage and started it downwards. Halfway down the shaft, at a point above the rooftop entrance, he halted the cage. Then he soared back up by means of his gravpak.

Quiroga was startled when he returned. Broward explained. "Maybe they can get enough men with paks underneath it to drive it back up. There are a lot of maybe's. There's work to do, and I'm helping with it."

They hammered furiously and then used the screwdrivers and a little crowbar to pry the lock mechanism out. Each expected something drastic to happen; both were sweating far more than the work alone could account for.

Then, the lock was out, and the wires connected to it were exposed. Quiroga began to make the necessary connections, but Broward did not wait for him to finish. He had been more worried about attack from the shaft than he had shown.

He looked down the rock walls. The light glared on the cage; it was moving upwards slowly. Smiling grimly, he rose over the hole and plunged downward. On reaching the cage, he turned the gravpak controls to give him half-weight. The barrel of his burper went over the edge at an angle so that the bullets would strike below the cage. He pressed the trigger, and the shaft became a deafening hell. Not so deafening that he could not hear the screams of the men below. Although they would have received no direct hits from the bullets themselves, they were undoubtedly wounded by fragments of stone chipped off the walls and sent flying.

He quit firing and looked over the edge through the space between the cage and the shaft. Below him, light flooded through the opened rooftop door. Men flew through it, out of the shaft and onto the top of the building. Some were still screaming.

He fired at an Angel halfway through the door, saw the body blow apart, and fired at the man behind it. That man fell fast because the bullets had destroyed his gravpak.

Their next move would be to bring in a mobile laser and burn the elevator down. Before that happened, the ship must be activated. He rose, leaving the elevator where it was, and returned to Quiroga.

The lieutenant said, "I was worried. I heard the shots."

"Just a little holding action. It won't keep long. Any luck?"

"It isn't trapped. Howards must not have thought that anybody would find it. We're ready to go. See that button there? I think it's the emitter control. Anyway, it's the only one whose function I don't know."

"Press it."

Quiroga shut the port of the ship first, then depressed the button. Slowly, a section of wall in front of the ship slid aside. Where it had been was a sheet of plastic. Quiroga kept his finger on the button, and the sheet slid in behind the rock section to reveal a tunnel. At its end was another plastic sheet.

Quiroga lifted the vessel slowly and piloted it into the tunnel. On its clearing the entrance, the plastic sheet slid back out of the wall. They waited until the exterior sensory of the ship indicated that the air had been pumped out of the tunnel. Again, Quiroga pressed the button. The sheet before them disappeared into the wall, then the rock behind it slid aside.

They were looking out on early morning Mars.

A yellowish-red plain stretched out to the horizon. Nothing moved on it, for Mars had no surface life, animal or vegetable. Far off to the left was a thin cloud of yellowish dust. Though it was day, the sky was a blackblue, the brighter stars filtered through the weak light of the small sun. Around the hill, they knew, would be the three big domes on top of Osorno.

"Take her out," Broward said. "Just far enough to turn her around. Then use the emitter to open the outer ports."

"*Dios mio!* Are you crazy?"

"I know exactly what I'm doing," Broward replied.

Quiroga shrugged, rolled his eyes upwards, and obeyed. In a few seconds, the false section of the hill and the plastic gate behind it had moved into the rock.

"Take her into the tunnel. But only halfway. I don't want the outer ports closing."

The Argentinean said something under his breath, but he drove the ship to the spot indicated.

"This ship has a burner laser," Broward said. "Use it."

Quiroga placed his hand over his face and groaned, "Stupid! Now I see what you mean to do. But . . ."

"You have a better idea?" said Broward.

"God help me, no."

Quiroga activated the laser, and a pencil-thin white beam shot out of the nose of the craft and bore through the plastic. Then, Quiroga described a large circle with the beam. The plastic resisted only breifly, bubbled, then disappeared. Quiroga shut the beam off, moved the ship forward swiftly and bumped into the center of the described circle. While the ship was backing up to its original position, the large disc of plastic fell out of the sheet and onto the rock floor.

The laser struck again. This time, the thick granite section held out longer. But there was air pushing against it from the other side. Suddenly, the slab of rock, marked by a thin dark line where the laser had cut, began to move outwards.

"Back! Back!" said Broward loudly, but Quiroga had already touched the controls. The ship shot out of the tunnel at a velocity that would have crushed the two of them if they had not been in stasis.

They went back a long ways, and they needed the distance, for the granite disc came out of the mouth of the tunnel like a bullet out of the muzzle of a gun. It did not fly far after that but, when it hit the surface of the hill on its edge, it turned over once. Then, instead of falling flat, it landed on its opposite edge and began rolling down the slope like the hoop of a giant child.

The two men did not watch it run its course. They were too fascinated, and shocked, though they had expected it, at what followed the disc. A man, upside down, flew out of the tunnel. Another came behind him, then the water tank and the provisions chest. Two men, holding on to each other. A fifth Angel. Then, the elevator cage.

Broward and Quiroga could not see it, but they could imagine the roar of the thick air escaping from Osorno through the cave and the shaft that led down to Howards' house and the plaza on the third level. Dust blew up from the hill, a yellow-red cloud that obscured the tunnel. Abruptly, a door soared out from the tunnel and flopped on the plain. The door at the entrance to the house at the bottom of the shaft?

Quiroga spoke with a choking voice. "It must be hell down there. The people fighting to get out of the plaza before the barriers come down in the tunnels at each end and seal them off. But they can't do anything but roll before the great wind until they are smashed against a wall and held there. Or slide along until the wind carries them through the doors and broken windows into the house and maybe even up the shaft."

He put his hands over his face. "I do not weep for Howards and his men, because they deserve to die. But there are innocent people in that plaza. Women and children, Mier's daughter . . ."

Broward put his hand on the lieutenant's shoulder. "I am sorry, deeply sorry. What else can I say? Now, would you take the ship back in? We'll close the outer ports; they should be strong enough to take the wind. Once they're closed, your people can start pumping air back into the plaza.

"And buck up. You've got a lot of explaining to do and a lot of organizing. You're not going to get much sleep. Neither will I. I have to get back to Deimos. But I'll be coming back."

Quiroga stood up, tears running down his face, and said, "I'll put on my suit."

Broward did not reply. He was so tired that he wanted to do nothing but sleep.

Four Mars days later, he left the red planet again, headed this time for the Moon. Quiroga, spokesman for the Martians, sat beside him. Below them, on the dwindling reddish ball, the newly formed government was trying to determine the course of its society. After the outbreak against the more devoted followers of Howards, most of whom had been killed by those eager for revenge as soon as the news of El Macho's death was known, a temporary government had been set up.

Labastida, an admiral, and Learmont, one-time mayor of Osorno, had been released from the prison where Howards had recently placed them. After hearing Broward's story, they had agreed that he should return to the Moon. He was to attempt to arrange for a truce. Eventually, they hoped, a treaty would be made. Peace could be established, and the survivors could get down to the serious and harsh business of struggling for a living and of hewing out of the subarean and sublunarian rock *Lebensraum* for themselves and their descendants.

Broward had sent the bomb in an orbit towards the sun. It was traveling at top speed towards its fiery tomb; nothing could divert or recall it.

Now, Quiroga was with him as ambassador. Since he alone had any acquaintance with the Moonman, and since he had several important relatives, he had gotten the job.

The two did the things that a man must do to keep from going mad during the long voyage in cramped quarters. However, for Broward, the return was not as bad as the original trip. He had someone to talk to.

Quiroga said, "This Athenian ideology or philosophy you mentioned? What is it?"

Broward smiled and said, "Once, I would have been very eager to explain it to you. I'd have talked for hours on end and only reluctantly dropped the subject. But not now."

"But what is it?"

"Briefly, it was the idea of setting up human government and society so that all was decentralized. Well, not everything. With the huge and crowded population Earth had, there were many things that could only be handled by a terrestrial-wide government.

"But I wanted society cut into the minimum segments possible. Each segment would be composed of, say, five hundred men and women. These would govern all local affairs, and the governing would be conducted on a basis like that which ancient Athens had.

"This would require, of course, a politically educated and zealous electorate. I wasn't naive enough to think that people would naturally be so. However, the idea was that the children would be educated to be so, conditioned, as it were."

"And who would enforce this conditioning, this education?"

"There you are. The weak point. Or one of them. Only a powerful central government could make this come about. And such a government is not likely to bring about its own demise wilfully. In a way, I had the same idea as Marx himself. That is, he thought the state would wither away after a world government was established and the proletariat ruled. That idea, though still paid lip service to by our leaders and taught in school, had been abandoned in practice. Only the most diehard Marxist subscribed to it.

"Unconsciously, I must have been affected by what my teachers offered me, even though not many of them believed it. Long after I had conceived the Athenian ideology, I realized my error. However, by then, I had formed my Athenian Underground. It was absurd to think that the authorities didn't know of it. They did, but they allowed me to go unharmed, even to be given a place of trust on the Moon. Why? I don't know for sure. Perhaps, they were using me to detect other potential subversives. At any time they wanted to, they could have brought the entire movement, which was small, anyway, to its knees by using the bone-phones.

"Later, I realized this, too. But it was too late to back out. So, I went ahead as if I had not been detected. If the authorities were willing to let me play my little game, I was willing. Though I lost much of my enthusiasm.

"Then, when most of Earth was killed, and human society was suddenly restricted, I began thinking again. Now, Athenianism could work. And the children would be so few in numbers, they could easily be educated. They would grow up thinking that the Athenian system of democracy was the best way for men to govern themselves. All would be free, within necessary limits, of course. The old would be kicked out; the new, based on rationality and logic, would come in."

He fell silent for a while. Quiroga shifted around in his seat, then said, "And now?"

Broward shrugged, and said, "I think I've learned. Man is only logical when he is working with machines or mathematics or in the laboratory. And not always then. Otherwise, he behaves as custom demands. Oh, there are men who don't, and enough of these at one time influence society to change its customs, though slowly. Or technological changes influence them to adopt new customs. But these changes are not made systematically or after much thought. They just come about.

"The born conservative resists them; the born liberal adopts them. Neither knows quite why he resists or adopts, though he gives rational reasons for his conduct. Then, they die, and the same process goes on with their sons and their sons' sons. And so it goes."

"You've given up?"

"No. I can't. Even realizing the truth, I can't. Besides, now that mankind is so few, one man's feelings and ideas may wield great power. But I'm not going to try to change society overnight. I'll do my best to introduce what I think are good ideas. If they're rejected, I won't kill or jail people for it."

"This Scone?" Quiroga said. "He will kill. He will kill you because you disobeyed him and threw away his chance for victory."

"Scone is a man like Genghis Khan, Napoleon, Hitler. He has no business existing in this world. He'd like to keep the old order, with himself as top dog, of course. He's reactionary down to his bones, yet he's a great fighter, a soldier who won't stop until his enemy is dead or he's dead. So . . ."

He continued, "I've been thinking about a plan to inform the people on the Moon of what's happened without Scone being able to repress the news. I'm also informing them about the surplus of women on Mars and your people's offer to send volunteer women to the Moon to balance out the lack there. That's a very strong point. If you'll excuse me, I'll get to work on that now."

He spent several hours in recording, wiping out, re-recording. Finally, he was satisfied. Then, for the relay satellite had been contacted a little while before, he transmitted. Over and over again.

"And what do you expect to happen?" said Quiroga. He had been listening quietly but with some puzzlement while Broward talked into the mike.

"This message will be taped at the Moon receiving station," he answered. "The operator will also listen in. He won't understand a word of it, of course, because it's in Navaho. He won't even know what language it is. There'll be an uproar; he'll call in Scone. Scone will summon Dahlquist, because he's the man most likely to understand an exotic language. Dahlquist will listen, and the first thing he'll hear will be my request that he not tell Scone the truth.

"That's one of the weak points in my plan. If Dahlquist won't go along, then we're done for. But I know him; I'm banking on him. If he does as I say, he'll tell Scone that I've lost the codebook and am using Navaho for communication. It's just as good as any code.

"What he won't tell Scone—I hope—is that Mars is not bombed and that it's suing for peace. He'll tell those he can rust, and he'll tell Ingrid. At least she'll know I'm coming back and that she can hope. After that, well . . ."

"Very clever," the Martian said. "But this Scone is also very clever, crafty as a wolf, and he has great power. He may not believe what this Dahlquist tells him."

"He probably won't. But he surely won't dare to use force on the old Swede. Dahlquist is a very respected and much loved man."

"What if Scone decides not to take a chance but sends a ship to intercept and destroy us before we get there? His most faithful henchmen would do that for him, wouldn't they? And if nothing was said about it, everybody on the Moon would think you had had some accident. Ships disappear all the time, you know, and nothing is ever heard of them again."

"That's a chance we'll have to take," Broward said. "I doubt if Scone would do that. Why should he? He thinks that everything he's wanted has come about. He can easily deal with me once I land—he thinks."

Nevertheless, Broward was very uneasy after this. He kept expecting the alarms of the ship to sound out, to indicate that a UFO had been picked up by the radar. He did some calculation. If Scone sent a ship after him several hours after he'd received the message, then it should be within radar area in about five hours from now.

He sat tensely until the five hours had passed. Still, he did not relax. The interceptors might have left later. Six hours, seven, eight, passed. He sighed with relief. Although it was still possible that a ship might appear, the possibility dwindled the closer the scout came to the Moon. Scone would not want the lunar detectors to witness the explosion that would result if the interceptor blew him up with a small atomic bomb.

But there was the very good probability that the Moon no longer had any missiles. The last battle with the Axe fleet would have expended them, since there were few when the fight started. Mars itself had no more than three left.

If that were the case, the interceptor would use beams. Well, if he detected a UFO coming at him, and he'd do so before it was within a half-million mile range, he'd take evasive action. This would not be like the evasive action taken by airplanes during the old wars on Earth. Even though the occupants of spaceships were not affected by sudden angles of flight or decelerations or accelerations, the ships had their limits. No, he would simply place the ship in a new orbit shortly before it came within effective range of the lasers. At the speed the interceptor would be going, it could not turn around in time to catch him before he had reached the Moon. Unless, of course, the interceptors were lucky and caught him with a wild swing of the beams.

Hours passed, and no strange ship appeared ahead of him. So, Scone did not intend to destroy him before he reached home base. Probably, so egotistical was Scone, he did not think it necessary. He had used Broward for his own purposes despite Broward's feeling, and he would now dispose of him when and as he wished.

Broward began worrying about another thing. Why hadn't Scone answered his message?

He told Quiroga this latest thought, and the Martian said, "Why should he?"

Two more hours were rounded off on the ship's chronometer. Then, a message did come. But it was only a routine acknowledgment of Broward's approach and directions on where to land.

There were still six hours to go to landing time. Since he was now close enough to lock in and to use laser channels for communication, and the need for code was gone, he asked the operator the news.

"Sorry, Captain," replied the operator. "Just follow orders."

Angry, frustrated, Broward did not make another attempt. Even seeing the great globe of earth and the smaller one of its satellite ever expanding before him did not make him feel any better. What was going on down there?

At the designated time, the scout landed before the entrance lock to the port of Clavius. This was a new tube that had been extended from the ruins of the old base. Near it loomed the gigantic cigar-shaped *Zemlya*. Several men in suits were working on the stern of the vessel. Occasionally, one of them ventured from the shadows into the sunlit areas to work a little while before retreating. Even now, the problems of keeping a suit cool in the full heat of the sun had not been solved. But the repairs on the *Zemlya* seemed to have been all but completed. Even as Broward and Quiroga left their craft, the figures dropped off the scaffolding and descended slowly to the surface. They then walked to a port near the stern and entered.

Broward and Quiroga were also in suits, since the lock was not fitted for direct attachment to a ship and a force field was not being generated due to lack of power. Quiroga, speaking through his radio, said, "I feel very strange. And, though I should not admit it, I am afraid. It is like entering a cave of wolves."

"Some of those wolves are my friends," Broward said. "And they want peace as much as you do, I'm sure. Don't worry. Whatever happens, I won't desert you. You have my word."

He pressed the button that opened the lock from the outside, after looking through the transparent shield to make sure that no one was within. Normally, the locks had features built within them to ensure that they could not be opened unless it was safe for those inside the lock. But materials were so scarce now, and the lock had been built so swiftly, that Broward was not sure that regular precautions had been taken.

The lock was empty. The port swung open; they stepped inside; the port closed. Air soon filled the little chamber, and the two then opened the inner port and went down a narrow shaft. There was no ladder; they had to fall down the approximately 3.1 meters.

Beneath the shaft was a larger room and a tunnel that led to a still larger. Both rooms had racks on which were suits and associated equipment, but this had several desks. Presumably, these were to be used by the officials who checked men in and out. Now, they were deserted.

"That's strange," said Broward, then he stiffened. He had heard gunshots.

Broward said, "That can mean only one thing. But I don't know who'll be coming down that tunnel in a minute."

"We have no guns," said Quiroga. "Let's go back to the ship."

Broward did not answer but whirled and ran through the other room and leaped up the shaft. At the entrance to the lock, he quickly replaced and resecured his helmet. Quiroga did the same. They entered the lock and, without waiting for the air to be pumped out, went out onto the lunar plain. Behind them, the escaping atmosphere pushed, but they jumped up and allowed it to sail them towards their ship.

In the scout, Broward seized a burper and handed another to Quiroga.

"Back to the shaft," he said.

They made it just in time. The barks of larger caliber weapons and the pop-pop of smaller guns came up through the shaft. Then, there was a silence. Broward guessed that, whoever they were down there, they were putting on suits. And their antagonists had, for some reason, stopped firing.

He said to Quiroga, "If it's Dahlquist and his men, we'll simply help them make for the *Zemlya*. If it's Scone, we'll stop them. He'll be trying for the *Zemlya*, too."

Below him, a man appeared. The fellow looked up before jumping, and Broward recognized him as Radman, the commander of the *Zemlya*. At the same time, Radman saw him. He cried out and raised his .20 centum. Broward threw himself back and on the floor to escape the stream of explosives. The ceiling above the shaft broke into a thousand chips and went flying around the top of the shaft and back down it.

When the thum-thum of the little exploding bullets had quit, Broward rolled near the shaft. He called out, "Radman! I want to speak to Scone!"

There was a silence. Seconds passed, a minute. Then Scone's voice came hollowly up the shaft.

"Broward! You bad penny! I underestimated you by far! But you haven't won yet!"

Broward shouted back, "Why not?"

Scone's voice was triumphant. "Because I have Ingrid Nashdoi!"

Broward gritted his teeth and said, "How do I know you have her?"

"I picked her up while we were fighting our way out to here. I knew she'd be handy as a hostage. Besides, I want her!"

"I think you're bluffing."

Scone did not answer. Broward wondered what he would do next. Perhaps, he and Quiroga should go out to the scout. They could place it against the lock and beam down anybody who tried to come out.

A scream wailed up through the shaft. Broward stiffened and cursed. He cursed again when he heard Ingrid's voice crying out in agony.

Immediately thereafter, Scone shouted up, "Now do you believe?"

"All right," Broward replied. "Now what?"

"I just want to get to the *Zemlya*," Scone said. "I know you've got me cornered. So, I'll make a trade with you. Ingrid for the *Zemlya*."

Broward did not need to ask what Scone would do if he

were turned down. He'd try to fight his way out, even if he knew it was hopeless. But he'd kill Ingrid first.

"There's been too much bloodshed already," said Broward. "Most of it entirely needless. All right. You can have the *Zemlya*. But release Ingrid first."

"What kind of a fool do you think I am?" Scone replied.

"Scone, the *Zemlya* will be a small price to pay to get rid of you and your kind. Believe me, I want you to leave on it. Release her, and on my word, I'll do nothing to prevent you from escaping. More, I'll do my best to see that no one on the Moon goes after you."

Again, there was silence. Though it was cold by the shaft, Broward was sweating.

He turned to Quiroga. "Take the scout. Melt all the destructive projection equipment you can locate on the exterior of the *Zemlya*. I doubt if those in it will know about it; they're not likely to have the sensories on. Come back as soon as you're through, and park the ship to one side. Have the beams ready to go if I give the word or if I don't come out with the others."

Quiroga nodded and left. Broward said loudly down the shaft, "What about it, Scone? You don't have much choice, you know. You have to trust me."

There were several shots, an exchange between Scone's group and the others, he hoped. Then Scone said, "You lucky bastard! To show up just at the right time for you, wrong time for me."

Broward replied, "Sure!" But he was thinking that it might not, perhaps, be all luck. Too many things had happened. The finding of the undersea colony off Yakan and then the submarine station off Israel where Moshe and Katashkina had started a new life and a new nation. Then, his finding and rescue of Quiroga and the events it had led to, including the discovery of the escape shaft of Howards and the consequent defeat of Howards. And now, almost as if it had been arranged, his arrival at the lock just before the fleeing Scone.

"Throw your weapons onto the floor of the shaft," he said. "Come up one by one. I'll let you through the lock in groups of three."

There was a clatter as a burper struck the rock floor. Scone followed it. He raised his huge stone-statue face upwards, grinned slightly, and leaped. Broward, who had risen, stepped back, his gun held on the big man.

"So you win," said Scone. "For the time, at least. I won't be back, but my descendants will some day."

"They may not be of the same mind as you," Broward replied. "Tell them to send Ingrid up. I want to be sure she's all right."

Scone shouted back down the shaft. In a few seconds, Ingrid was beside Broward. She was pale and shaking, but she managed to smile at him. In one hand she held Scone's burper.

A second man followed, then a woman.

Ingrid said, "Olga's a prisoner. They took her along when they came across her in the corridors. She doesn't want to go."

Broward motioned to the woman to step behind them. Scone said, "Wait a minute. We can't go without women."

"The tanks of the *Zemlya* have women," said Broward. "You can thaw them out."

Scone licked his lips and looked for a second as if he were going to jump Broward. But, seeing the expression on Broward's face, he stepped back.

Another man came up. He joined the first two, and they entered the lock. Broward, looking past them through the transparent ports, saw that the scout was still busy burning off the beam apparatus.

Scone, of course, would know what he was doing. Doubtless he was furious. But he would also know that his last chance for attack was gone. He could do nothing but take off for the stars.

There were three other groups, the last of which contained four because of an extra person, a woman. Broward watched this head towards the *Zemlya*. By then, Scone had disappeared inside the great ship.

A few minutes after the final group had entered and the port was closed, the *Zemlya* lifted. None of the men working on the ship had come out. Either Scone had forced them to go along with him or else they had volunteered. The latter, probably, since Scone would have trusted none but loyal followers with the *Zemlya*.

Ingrid broke down and wept for a long time. When she had recovered herself, she said, "I thought it was all up, that I'd never see you again. Dahlquist and some of his friends came to arrest Scone. He was in a conference with his deputies. These surrendered, but not Scone. He shot two of the men with Dahlquist and led his deputies to an arsenal. He

new he was too outnumbered to fight the whole colony, so
e decided to escape on the *Zemlya*, find a new world in the
tars. But he took me out of my cell, said he was going to
eepfreeze me, thaw me out when he found a planet. But
e wouldn't have gotten me. I would have killed myself first
hance . . ."

Broward patted her back and said, "I know, sweetheart.
ry to forget what's happened, think of it as a nightmare.
Iow, we're awake and in a world that needs to be gardened
nd needs love as never before."

But he was looking through the port. Outside, in the garish
unlight, the *Zemlya* was only a spark. He thought, a spark
urns inside that spark. Scone. A spark to set the stars
fire. God help the people of the world he might some day
nd.